"You lead a very privileged life, Sally. Do you know that?"

"What do you mean?"

"That fancy apartment, the farm, the horses, the convertible."

"I know that," she said defensively. "Don't think I don't appreciate it. I never lived like this before Uncle Hal came along. Sometimes I feel quite guilty about it."

"Maybe you're doing something you shouldn't. People don't usually feel guilty for no reason."

Sally just looked at John, trying to figure out what he meant. Was that a dig about leading him on, then suddenly freezing up? He was a fine one to talk! He was doing a lot worse than that.

"Maybe I'm not the only one who should feel guilty...."

Dear Reader,

Blue skies, sunshine, the scent of fresh-cut grass, a walk on the shore—some summer pleasures are irresistible. And Silhouette Romance has six more to add to your list—this month's irresistible heroes who will light up your August days—or nights—with romance!

He may act like a man of steel, but this FABULOUS FATHER has a heart of gold. Years of separation had made Gavin Hunter a stranger to his son, yet he was determined to make his home with the boy. But with beautiful Norah Bennett standing in his way, could Gavin win his son's heart without losing his own? Find out in Lucy Gordon's *Instant Father.*

Our next hero can be found in Elizabeth August's own SMYTHESHIRE, MASSACHUSETTS. Ryder Gerard may have married Emily Sayer to protect her young son, but he never intended to fall in love. *A Wedding for Emily* weaves the mysterious legacy of Smytheshire with the magic of marital love.

No reader will be able to resist the rugged, enigmatic Victor Damien. In Stella Bagwell's *Hero in Disguise,* reporter Sabrina Martin sets out to discover what her sexy boss, Victor, has to hide. Sabrina always gets her story, but will she get her man?

For more wonderful heroes to spend these lazy summer days with, check out Carol Grace's *Mail-Order Male,* Joan Smith's *John Loves Sally* and exciting new author Pamela Dalton's *The Prodigal Husband.*

In the coming months, we'll be bringing you books by all your favorite authors, such as Diana Palmer, Annette Broadrick, Marie Ferrarella, Carla Cassidy and many more.

Happy reading!

Anne Canadeo
Senior Editor

JOHN LOVES SALLY

Joan Smith

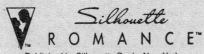

Silhouette
ROMANCE™
Published by Silhouette Books New York
America's Publisher of Contemporary Romance

SILHOUETTE BOOKS
300 East 42nd St., New York, N.Y. 10017

JOHN LOVES SALLY

ISBN: 0-373-08956-2

First Silhouette Books printing August 1993

Printed in the U.S.A.

JOAN SMITH

has written many Regency romances, but likes working with the greater freedom of contemporaries. She also enjoys mysteries and Gothics, collects Japanese porcelain and is a passionate gardener. A native of Canada, she is the mother of three.

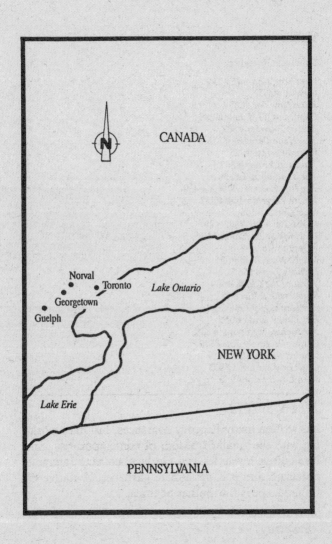

Chapter One

Sally Glover lifted her glass of champagne and clinked it against her Uncle Hal's glass. "To Theodosia," he said, and they drank.

There was not much physical resemblance between uncle and niece. Hal Harmon was a slender, elegant man, still handsome in his mid-fifties. He looked like an actor and talked like one. His accent had some trace of England, although he was an American. His sleek cap of silver hair contrasted magnificently with his weathered complexion. He was permanently tanned from his years in the Middle East as an undercover agent for the CIA. His tweed jacket, the nutmeg color of Devon's moors in autumn, and his custom-made ankle boots were his concession to having turned farmer. And the patches on the elbows of his jacket were to indicate he was also a professor. He taught a class in interntional marketing at Guelph University.

Sally thought he had probably looked distinguished even when he was disguised as a camel herder in the desert years ago, with a rag wrapped around his head.

"A million and a half bucks! Not a bad price for one cow," she said. "That's three hundred and seventy-five thou per udder."

Hal grimaced. "I admire your arithmetic, my dear, but your language leaves something to be desired. Must we speak of udders? And let me remind you, Theodosia is not just any cow. She is a thoroughbred prize-winning holstein from Hilltop Farm, the best holstein breeding farm in the country, if I do say so myself."

"Like I said, a cow," Sally grinned. She enjoyed teasing her debonair uncle. She suspected that he enjoyed these little lectures, too. He was her mother's brother, but no one would ever guess it to see them. They had been born on a dairy farm in Wisconsin, but her mom married a Canadian school teacher and settled down in a small city in Canada, while Hal had gone off to Washington and eventually become that creature of legend, a spy.

Sally had been in her last year at Guelph University when her dad retired, and he and her mom had moved to the West Coast. Her Uncle Hal had shown up the next year. She had been happy to move in with him. It was nice to have some family around again. He had bought this swell condo near the university in Guelph, and Hilltop Farm on the edge of Georgetown, thirty odd miles away. Although he was no longer a spy, he still kept his past a secret from everyone except family and a few close friends.

Hal reached out a slender hand and ruffled the nest of coppery curls atop her head. "Hoyden," he laughed. "We shall never make a proper countess of you. Yet you do remind me vaguely of Countess Sophia, one of my colleagues in my early spying days, when I worked in Eastern Europe. She had the same green, tilted, cat eyes, and the same full cheeks, tapering to a small chin. Sophia didn't have that smattering of freckles, nor your boyish figure, however. She was a lush, Rubenesque lady."

He sighed in memory, and took another sip of champagne from the tulip glass. Sally knew he missed Sophia and the old glory days of working in the field. The Silver Fox, they had called him. His hair had turned silver at thirty. As time caught up with him, he wanted a slower pace of life and had turned to cattle breeding, like his father before him.

His spying adventures now were all vicarious. Under the nom de plume of Hugo VanAark, he wrote madly successful spy-adventure novels, featuring the dashing Dirk Ransom and his assistant, Countess Sophia de Mornay. Sally thought it was a shame he wouldn't let his publisher put his picture on the back cover. It would have sold thousands more books.

The real Countess Sophia Hagershurt was long dead. An assignation gone wrong, a foe mistaken for a friend in the shadows of some European spa, and a bullet in the heart. Sally thought she would have enjoyed to know her memory lived on in fiction. Since Hal had broken his leg in that last tumble from a camel, he lacked the agility necessary for Dirk's exploits, and used Sally to test the various contrivances his plot called for. It was these forays into imaginary crime that earned Sally her nickname of Countess.

Hal prided himself on the feasibility of his plots. He had told her a dozen times if a thing was physically impossible, it didn't go into a Hugo VanAark book. That, and the realistic details from his firsthand experiences, were what made his novels a little special. Special enough that he now earned a seven-figure advance, and that was before the inevitable movie rights.

"You like it, Countess?" he asked Sally, nodding at the champagne.

She took another sip and smacked her lips. "Dee-licious."

"Ignoramus! This is an inferior *cru,* from a bad year."

She glanced at the bottle. "It's French."

"There is French, and there is *French.* I'm saving the Dom Pérignon '57 for the signing of my next contract. *After the Storm* is about ready to go. I have to decide on the final climax, and I want to read it once more to check for typing errors."

"This is the first time you've done a sequel, isn't it, Hal? I mean you always use Dirk and the Countess, but all the other characters and the setting in the Middle East are the same this time, too."

"The fortuitous timing of Desert Storm just after my book, *Before the Storm,* came out, demanded a sequel," he explained. "They do say, you know, that my book accounts for the name given the war by the media."

Sally took this with a grain of salt. Hal was good, but she hardly thought he was that good.

"We haven't heard the last of the boys in the Middle East," he continued. "I hope the White House reads my new opus. They might have saved the taxpayers a billion dollars a day if they'd heeded the warning in *Before the Storm.* My books are so well researched that the CIA is interested. They suspect I have illicit Eastern contacts. My last book *did* prophecy Desert Storm with meticulous accuracy, of course. I could have told the President—but never mind.''

''Why didn't you just phone the White House? They'd listen to the Silver Fox.''

''You know perfectly well I've severed all connection with Washington,'' Hal said. ''That's why I moved to Canada. It was the only way I could get any peace. They hound one to death. In fact, I set about a rumor that I'm dead. It cost me my pension, but they were being too bothersome. Between my farm and my books, I don't mind contributing that mite to my country. My publisher tells me the foreign secretary has requested an advance copy of my next novel, so he'll know my views.''

''But he doesn't know you're the author. He'd pay more attention if he knew it was the Silver Fox writing.''

''Leave the politics to me, child. You just write what I dictate.''

Sally shook her head. She loved her uncle, but there was no denying he liked to take all the credit for things. He called her his secretary, but she did a lot more than type! She contributed plenty of ideas to his books. Dirk Ransom had become a lot more popular since she had insisted on his having a love interest, to humanize him. In fact, she hadn't cared much for the first book at all. It was the introduction of the Countess, and romance, that stirred her interest.

Sally did all her uncle's business correspondence, kept him up-to-date on new fashions in clothes and foods and things. As for computers! Hal was scared stiff of them. She was in complete charge of his computer room.

"You're a confirmed male chauvinist pig, Hal. No wonder you could never get any woman to marry you," she said, and topped off her glass. "I like this inferior wine," she added.

"Your education has been sadly neglected, my dear. Now, about the climax for *After the Storm*. We must contrive a means of blowing up the Fat Man's limousine. An explosion makes such a satisfying background for the final clinch—you will like that, Sally. You always insist on a closing kiss. And the movie people will want it, too."

"The Fat Man's car is guarded when he's at home, so it would have to be after he's driven somewhere," Sally said.

"You're learning! Actually he's attending an OPEC meeting. We want a public place. Any suggestions where we could try out the action?"

"Someplace where the Fat Man will be staying a long time, so the chauffeur leaves the car unattended. Someplace where he feels the car is safe from Dirk Ransom."

"He is never safe from Dirk Ransom." Hal smiled.

Sally knew it would be her job to test the planting of the bomb in the limo. So what they wanted was some public place where she could simulate planting a bomb in a limousine. She knew Hal would choose the most difficult car to bomb, to heighten the danger in his novel.

"A piece of cake," she said. Hal winced at such crude slang. "An official function. The International Environment Conference starts tomorrow at the university. Since you're giving that class on international marketing, you got an invitation.'' Sally handled his mail, too.

"I abhor conferences. So much time is wasted listening to each member mount his own particular hobbyhorse."

"I meant the get-acquainted cocktail party at night. Your invitation is for you and a guest. Looks like a job for Countess Sophia."

"Excellent!"

"Plastic explosive under the hood, right? I'll take my Silly Putty."

"And your pearl-handled pistol. A spy never goes out unarmed. Especially a pretty female spy. The Countess has amorous men to deal with, as well as would-be assassins."

"I haven't noticed any excess of amorous guys, but I'll pack my realistic toy gun. It's a pain in the neck trying to squeeze that thing into my evening bag."

"That is exactly why I insist on your doing it. Accuracy, Sal. How should a man know the difficulties of a female spy? Realism is the key! Take the gun."

In Washington, the head of security, eastern branch, Roger Stynor, set down the phone and smiled in satisfaction. The Silver Fox was up to his old tricks, just as he suspected! Not dead, but gone underground in Canada. Breeding holsteins, of all things, and lecturing at some small-town university. He'd put a man on his tail immediately. Some sharp lad—John McCallum. He had handled himself superbly in Russia last year, when things were falling apart there.

He lifted his phone and said, "Can you come in for a minute, McCallum?"

John McCallum heard the buzz of excitement in his boss's voice and felt an answering flare of adrenaline course along his veins. "Be right there, boss." His instincts said, "Eastern Europe." He hauled his six-foot two-inch frame out of his chair and hurried along the hall.

Concentration pinched his craggy features into a frown. His tow hair was tousled from the fingers that plowed through it as he had sat at his desk, studying the latest reports from Eastern Europe. His broad shoulders, casual T-shirt, jeans and sneakers gave him the air of a college football player. But a closer look revealed a pair of warily mature blue eyes, and a few incipient wrinkles in his forehead.

"Can I help you, sir?" John asked his boss.

Staynor nodded to the leather chair beside his desk and John folded his long frame gracefully into it.

"We've just got a lead on Hal Harmon," Staynor said. "He disappeared four years ago, but he made the mistake of taking a teaching position at a university outside of the States. Ran out of money, I expect. He probably thought we'd lost interest. We were informed of it recently and requested that he be kept under surveillance. Now he's made contact with a certain Aswar Ranji, from the Middle East. One of his earlier contacts."

John blinked in confusion. "Hal Harmon? I don't think I recognize—"

"No, you wouldn't. He always used his nom de guerre. A bit full of himself, Harmon, but a first-rate man in the field. I'm talking about the Silver Fox."

John blinked in disbelief. "Good lord! The Silver Fox! I thought he was dead." The Silver Fox was a legend in the CIA. His cases were used as training material for new recruits. To John and others like him, he was the ultimate hero.

"That's what he wanted us to think. He had made a good many enemies. He's hiding out in Georgetown."

"Right on our doorstep? You said he moved outside the States."

"Not Georgetown, D.C. It's a small town in Canada, a suburb of Toronto. He used to live in Georgetown, Washington. No doubt he chose that town because of its name, the devil. He always had a bizarre sense of humor."

"When you say enemies, do you mean he turned coat?" John asked, his heart sinking. Another hero bites the dust.

"His loyalty was never in question when he was in the field, but it seems now he is still active—and he's *not* working for us. The Mounties ran a check on his bank account. It suggests he has more money than even his successful cattle-breeding farm can account for. *You* figure it out."

"You think he's sold out, then?"

"He left in a huff—some trouble over his pension. It could be he's taking revenge on us."

"What is it you want me to do?"

"Go to Georgetown and see what he's up to. He's a cagey old devil." He handed John a file. "This contains all the info we have. Residence—he has an apartment in a city called Guelph, where he teaches, and a dairy farm on the outskirts of Georgetown, called Hilltop Farm."

"It seems a pretty innocent sort of life," John said.

"He hasn't padded his bank account to seven figures with cows, McCallum. The farm is a fiendishly clever cover. He sells his cows all over the world and has potential buyers at his farm. This international marketing course he's teaching is another ruse that lends an innocent air to his correspondence abroad.''

John opened the file and glanced through it. Although he had been hearing of the Silver Fox for years, this was the first time he had seen a picture of him. A smile rose spontaneously to his lips. He looked exactly as a hero should look. Dashing, handsome, debonair, with a faint whiff of brimstone in his laughing eyes. John lifted the picture and found himself gazing at another photo, this one of a tousle-haired young woman.

''Who's the girl?'' he asked Staynor.

''The Silver Fox has got himself a vixen. Her name's Sally Glover. He calls her his niece,'' Staynor replied. His lifted brow indicated his opinion about the relationship. ''We're looking into it. Of course, Harmon was always a womanizer, and he didn't mind what age they were. There's definitely something fishy there. The Glover woman graduated in an honors language course from this Guelph University. The university offered her a fellowship to study for an M.A. She turned it down flat, moved in with Harmon and hasn't bothered looking for a job since.''

''The old goat!'' John said angrily. She looked like such a sweet kid. ''She's young enough to be his daughter.''

''That's another possibility. He never married, but she could be his illegitimate daughter, I suppose. You'll find everything you need in that file, McCallum. There's an international conference on the environment being held at Guelph University. It specializes in that sort of thing—also agriculture, veterinary medicine and so on.''

''What's my cover?''

''You're covering the convention for an American environment magazine. We'll call it the *Green Magazine*. I'll handle the paperwork—registering you at the convention, ID and so on. Unfortunately we have no photo of Ranji. If he's there, he may be using an alias. I'm sure Harmon will be there.''

''I don't know much about ecology,'' John said, biting his lip in concern.

''We'll try to drum up someone who does and send him along to join you. Don't worry about that. You just keep an eye out for the Fox, and the Middle Eastern delegates in particular. That's who Harmon will be seeing. Arrange some way to get a tour of Hilltop Farm while you're there. The Glover woman might be a possibility, but be careful of her. Don't go imagining she's some innocent young thing. Any cohort of Harmon's is trouble. My secretary will arrange for an advance for the trip. Keep in touch. With things heating up again in the east, this is top priority.''

John McCallum gathered up the papers and arranged for the advance. His fake ID and passport were ready in time for him to take the next flight from Washington to Toronto. On the plane he studied the information Stynor had given him, and the maps of the area. It must be pretty countryside. The farm was nestled in the Halton Hills, northwest of Toronto.

When he landed, he rented a car and drove directly to Guelph by Highway 401, the MacDonald-Cartier Freeway, missing the beauty of the hills of Halton. Guelph was a smallish city, about eighty thousand people. It seemed sedate and well behaved. The focal

point was a big stone Gothic church, or maybe cathedral, that sat high above the downtown.

John had memorized his map and headed for the
College Inn, where the delegates for the conference
were being put up. It was a brick building, not a high
rise, but it spread out in various wings with a series of
gabled roofs. It was just a stone's throw from the university. The hotel had a program for the conference.
He picked up one at the desk when he registered, and
went to his room for a quick shower. Then he headed
to the bar and studied the program while relaxing with
a beer.

He'd missed the opening meeting, which suited him
just fine. He was familiar with the flag-waving and
cliché talk that went on at opening meetings. He circled the next item on the program—9:00 p.m., Cock-
tails at Graham Hall. Get acquainted with delegates.
Would that require formal wear? Better get his black
jacket pressed.

He also circled a lecture at two-thirty the next afternoon. A panel discussion on the environmental
devastation caused in Kuwait by the uncapped wells
burning out of control. The Silver Fox wouldn't miss
that one! He wondered if Miss Glover would be there.
He had slipped her picture and the Silver Fox's into his
jacket pocket to study closely, so he'd be sure to recognize them.

At least that was the excuse he gave himself. But it
was only Sally's picture he drew out and gazed at.
Something in her impish smile tugged at his heart-
strings. She looked so open and innocent. Not at all
the kind of woman he pictured the Silver Fox falling
for. More like the kind he wished he could find for
himself.

Chapter Two

At nine o'clock that evening, Sally brushed out her coppery curls in front of the mirror. Her shower had left them shining and bouncy. She liked her hair, but wasn't so sure about that nose full of freckles that went with it. She hated the cakey feel of foundation makeup. A light dusting of power took the sharp edge from the freckles. A brush of tawny eye shadow to highlight the green of her eyes, a light feathery line under them to enhance their size, a daub of lipstick and she was ready to go. Hal had given her three different bottles of French perfume but she didn't bother using any of them. The scent was overpowering.

She stood back from the mirror to admire her new dress. Uncle Hal stinted on sharing the praise, but he was generous with the financial rewards of his work. She wouldn't have been able to afford clothes like this silvery, hip-hugging wisp of raw silk on a teaching assistant's salary, which was what she'd be restricted to if she'd taken that language fellowship the university had offered her. Hal had also given her the long, dangly silver filigree earrings she wore. He said he'd bought them for ten cents in a bazaar in the East, but they'd cost an arm in a jewelry store here.

Hal was waiting in the living room of their penthouse apartment on Gordon Street, overlooking the campus. The living accommodations were another bonus of working with Uncle Hal. They stayed in this spacious condo during the week, and on the weekends they usually went to Hilltop Farm.

Hal had a wide streak of the volupturary in his makeup. The apartment was probably based on some palace he'd visited during his long and varied career. A seraglio, maybe. The walls should have been off-white, to highlight his collection of Impressionist and Expressionist paintings, but he had them sponge-painted in a brick shade streaked with gold.

The paintings were so valuable that he'd had an elaborate security system installed to protect them. The rich jewel tones of Rouault, whose works looked like stained glass, stood out in sharp relief against the wide gilt frame. Sally didn't care much for the abstract German Expressionist works, wild abstract slashes of color, but she liked the Monet water garden and the Renoir of the girl with hair the same fiery color as her own.

Hal strolled in, the epitome of sophistication in an impeccably tailored black jacket, with his silver hair gleaming. A brandy glass was cupped in his palm to warm the drink. "One always drinks brandy at body temperature," he had told her. She didn't drink it at all. It tasted like turpentine.

"That rotgut'll kill you, Hal. Let's split," she said.

"For your information, young lady, this is not rot-gut—such vulgarity! It is cognac, the finest brandy, from the Charente *département* of southwestern France. Nectar of the gods." He finished his drink and set the glass down.

Mrs. Locum would remove and wash it. She was their live-in housekeeper, another perk of working for Hal.

"You're equipped for your job, Countess?"

"I have my Silly Putty and toy gun. And my gloves, to hide my fingerprints and make the job really awk-ward."

"Now if only we could inculcate some sense of propriety! Countess Sophia always carried a pair of white kid gloves. But I daresay those ugly cotton ones will do."

"I'll take my own wheels, if you don't mind, Hal," she said, as they went down in the elevator.

"Why should I mind? Now that you ladies have proclaimed your equality with the superior sex—"

"Hah! Superior my eye!"

"As I was saying when you so rudely interrupted, I expect there'll be some interesting females at this little party."

"Just hang your tie on the doorknob if you 'vant to be alone,'" she said, to tease him. She knew Hal en-joyed female company, but he never conducted his affairs at the apartment. He entertained women more sedately there. He was quite strict about setting his niece a good example of manners, if not morals.

"Actually, you'd do better to go with me. Then your young man will be able to drive you home," Hal suggested.

"Good point, if I'm lucky enough to meet a young man. Okay, you can drive me."

The doorman had Mr. Harmon's Porsche waiting. It was three years old but in perfect condition. Hal didn't flaunt his wealth, outside of his home. He insisted on the best, but thought it vulgar to go chasing after every new fashion. His suits were from Savile Row, but he wore them until they were just on the edge of being tatty. He had only one watch, not a flashy Rolex but a quiet Cartier tank watch. He had once admitted he followed the British aristocracy in his lifestyle: the best, but not too much of it, and not too new.

They drove through the warm spring night to the campus parking lot closest to Graham Hall.

"Which are we using for the Fat Man's car, Dirk?' Sally asked. They assumed the names of the fictional characters when they were on the job.

Hal scanned the lot and spotted a shiny black limo parked close to the hall. "That one," he said with an impish grin. "Can you handle it, Countess?" It was the most conspicuous car on the lot, and parked in full light. She knew he'd pick the hardest one!

"Can cats meow?" she replied cockily.

"Yes, and I know from firsthand experience they also scratch," he replied satirically, which told her was referring to women.

Sally looked around the parking lot to see how she'd plant the Silly Putty bomb. She recognized one of the students on parking duty. He'd been in her history class a few years ago and was working on his master's degree now. That could be useful. She made a point of speaking to him as they went in.

"Hi, Scotty! I see your higher education is being put to good use." She grinned.

"Hey, don't knock it. It only pays five bucks an hour, but the tips are great."

"Whose house on wheels is that?" She knew it was a government car from the license plate. She went and peered in at the window of the limo. A pile of papers was on the front seat. Sally looked closer. It was the opening speech from the conference.

Scotty said, "The Honorable Clyde Masters, the minister of the environment. He gave the opening address at the conference this afternoon. Nice to see how our tax dollars are being spent, huh?"

"One can hardly expect a cabinet minister to ride a bicycle," Hal said as he took Sally's elbow to lead her up the stairs. "Convenient, your knowing the carhop, Countess," he smiled. "You won't get the poor lad in trouble, I hope."

"You're a little mixed up, Hal. It's guys who get us women in trouble."

"Must you always be thinking of sex?"

"No, only when I'm awake."

"You're incorrigible!" he scolded, but he was smiling.

As they entered Graham Hall, a babble of voices rose up to the ceiling. A milling throng of bodies circulated in a vast room. Many of the men wore black jackets; the women wore colored gowns. A smattering of burnooses and headdresses made the contingent from the East easy to spot.

"I'm supposed to meet a certain gentleman," Hal said vaguely. "Can you look after yourself, Countess?"

"Piece of cake."

In the shadows of the far wall, John McCallum
stiffened to attention when he spotted the Silver Fox.
He could hardly believe he was in the presence of this
legend. Surely the man had not turned traitor! It was
like thinking Superman stole candy from babies. Then
his eyes slid to the redhead, and he felt an increase of
disillusionment. She looked so cute, so saucy, yet innocent. His eyes lingered on the wisp of silk hugging
her boyish body. She was shorter than he'd been picturing. She wouldn't reach his chin. There wasn't
much of her, but it was a neat package and expen-
sively wrapped.

Without wasting a moment, he began to weave his
way toward the couple. He heard the Fox call the
woman Countess. Countess? There was no way the
Fox's niece was a countess—unless she had married
some shady European count. That was possible, he
supposed , but she looked so young. More likely she
was the Silver Fox's mistress.

John stood a moment, wondering which of his sus-
pects to follow. The Silver Fox was going to the bar—
not much mischief he could get into there. He glanced
back at the woman. She seemed to be looking for
someone. He watched as she looked all around until
she had spotted the minister of the environment. She
lifted her chin and straightened her impertinent little
shoulders as if she meant business, and made a beeline for him. John edged closer and listened.

"Good evening, Mr. Masters," she said, with a pert
smile. She looked innocent, but she knew how to use
her charms. The minister was smiling. "I'm Sally
Glover, from the *Ontarian*—that's the students'
newspaper here on campus. I really enjoyed your
speech this afternoon. I wonder if I could have a copy

of it for the newspaper for those who weren't fortu-
nate enough to hear it. We have over twelve thousand
readers," she added, to entice him.

John listened in disbelief. She wasn't a student. She
was lying her head off! And doing it with an innocent
batting of her eyelashes that left the minister gaga.

"I don't have a copy on me," the minister said,
glowing in the rare luxury of praise from a voter. "I
have a copy in my car. Perhaps—"

"I wouldn't dare take you away from the party,"
she said. "But I do wish I could get a copy. Would you
trust me with the keys?" she asked, eyelashes working overtime. "I promise I won't steal your car."

"The parking lad has them. Tell him I said it was all
right, Miss—"

"Glover. Sally Glover. Thanks so much."

She turned and headed to the door, with John hot
at her heels. Now what the devil was she up to? The
minister had some secret documents in his car, and she
meant to walk away with them! Really, these politi-
cians had no sense.

He followed Sally out, noticing she slid on a pair of
gloves as she went. Highly suspicious! The minister's
car was parked close to the building. She spoke to the
car park.

"Hi, Scotty. The Honorable Masters said I can have
a copy of his speech. It's on the front seat. Mind
opening his car for me?"

"He told me to watch it closely," Scotty replied
uncertainly.

"Hey, you can watch me. I'm not planning to steal
it, you know."

"I'll get the speech myself. No harm in that. It's already been read in public. What do you want it for?"

"My uncle wants it," she said, since Scotty knew she didn't work for the paper.

Scotty opened the door on the driver's side. He had to move over to the far side to get the speech. Sally slid in beside him. "I've never been in one of these," she said, feigning enthusiasm. "I bet it has a bar in the back seat and everything."

While Scotty peered over the seat, she reached down and unlocked the hood, chatting to cover the sound.

"Sure enough," Scotty said. "Johnnie Walker—Black Label. The best."

"You're wasting your time studying history. You should run for member of parliament." She laughed.

He handed her a copy of the speech and they both got out. "Thanks, Scotty," she said, and turned to leave.

But when Scotty went to greet another celebrity car, she stayed behind. John McCallum watched, intrigued, as she quietly lifted the hood and put something under it, wearing those gloves to avoid fingerprints. Good Lord! She was a terrorist! She was planting a bomb! What nefarious scheme was the Silver Fox up to? Was it going to be an assassination? A kidnapping, with the bomb to create a diversion? What should he do?

Sally stuck the wad of Silly Putty on the side of the engine block and nodded in satisfaction. Then she thought of what officialdom would say when they found it there. It looked like a plastic explosive. There would be an investigation—Scotty would probably get in trouble. She took the Silly Putty and pushed it back into her purse. She had proved it could be done. That was all Hal cared about. She left and went back into Graham Hall, unaware that she had been observed.

John darted immediately to the car. The hood was still unlocked. He lifted it and peered inside. Nothing. He took out a flashlight and ran it over the whole engine bay. Nothing had been tampered with. No pulled wires. When he was convinced there was no bomb and no harm done to the engine, he began to reconsider what he had seen. If she hadn't planted a bomb, she must have taken something. Something had been hidden under the hood. And whatever it was, she had put it in her purse. He meant to get into her purse and discover what it was before the evening was over.

He went back into Graham Hall and peered around until he spotted a nest of Titian curls. There—she was at the bar, ignoring the hard liquor and calmly helping herself to a glass of punch. He wandered nonchalantly forward.

"Good evening," John smiled. "Nice party."

"Hi," Sally replied, running her eyes appreciatively over this stranger. Handsome! And well built, too. He had a football player's broad shoulders, and a nice, solid-looking face. Not flashy and devilishly handsome like Hal, but a strong nose and squarish chin that suggested a streak of stubbornness. She especially liked his blue eyes, and the way they crinkled at the corners when he smiled.

"I'm John McCallum," he said, offering his hand. She put her gloveless hand into it.

"I'm Sally Glover. You're an American?" she asked. She had caught a trace of Yankee in his voice. It was the way he said "evening," half swallowing the syllables. "Even'n," it sounded like.

"That's right."

"I guess you're an environmentalist, since you're at the conference."

"I'm covering it for an environmental journal. Journalism's really my field," he added, as he felt he didn't know as much about the environment as a specialist should. Best to explain his inadequacies before she discovered them.

"Maybe you'd like this," she said, and handed him the minister's opening speech, which she was finding a nuisance to carry.

"Why, thank you," he said, and accepted it. That proved the speech was only an excuse to get into the minister's car. "I owe you one," he added, smiling. "What's your interest in the conference, Miss Glover?"

"Call me Sally. I'll really not much interested. I mean I'm interested in the environment, naturally, but I can't claim to be an expert. I just recycle what I can and don't use spray cans. I'm not attending the lectures. I just came to the party with my uncle."

John looked vaguely around the hall. "Which lucky guy's your uncle?" he asked, with a lazy smile.

Sally saw the admiration in his eyes, and warmed to it. She didn't hesitate to point out Hal Harmon. "He teaches a course in marketing at the university. He's just here for the free booze, too," she said.

Yet John noticed Harmon was having his free drinks with a man in a burnoose. "You live in Guelph, then?"

"Yes, I was born here."

"Nice place."

After a few moments of conversation, they seemed to be getting on well. Sally agreed to take their drinks to the side of the room away from the traffic and find empty chairs to continue their meeting in comfort. They talked about the city, which had been founded by Scottish immigrants and was spotted with lovely old stone buildings.

"It's laid out like a European city," she explained. "Guelph was the original name of one of the royal houses of Europe. Hanover, I think," she added.

"I expect you've been to Europe?" he asked, eager to glean any crumbs.

"A couple of times. I like Italy—all that old art. I fell in love with Florence."

"Do you do a lot of traveling?" he asked, hoping to bring up the Middle East in an offhand way.

"Just one quick tour of England, France, Spain and Italy. Then in my holidays last year I went back to Italy."

"With your uncle?"

"No, my uncle and I aren't Siamese twins." She laughed. "I went with a friend. A girlfriend," she added, because she didn't want John to think she was fast.

He leaned a little closer and said, "Since you're not physically attached to your uncle, he won't mind if I steal you for a couple of hours. What do you say we split?"

Sally bit her lip in hesitation.

"The drinks will still be free," he promised. "We'll tell your uncle we're leaving." This would give him an excuse to meet the man her uncle was talking to. Was it Aswar Ranji?

She wanted to get to know him better. John seemed all right, but she didn't like that casual mention of drinks.

"Your uncle won't mind, will he?" John asked. He sensed her reluctance and felt she was afraid to leave with another man. This sign indicated she could indeed be Harmon's mistress.

"Who, Hal? Heck no, he won't care. It's just that— I hope I didn't give you the wrong impression. I don't usually go out with strange men," she said with a shy smile and suddenly looked about twelve years old.

"I'm not all that strange, am I?"

"I don't know. You seem nice."

"I am nice. You'll see." He smiled an honest, open smile, but he felt like Judas lying to her.

"Well, if you want to make that drink coffee, I guess it'd be all right. I've already had two glasses of punch. That's about my limit."

The punch had only a hint of liquor in it. She was either a complete innocent, being duped by the Silver Fox, or she was wily enough to play the ingenue to perfection. Since she had no reason to mistrust him, John decided she was innocent.

"I'm easy," he said. "Coffee it is. You choose the spot."

"How about my place?" she asked. Mrs. Locum would be in the apartment, if not the living room.

He was a little surprised at her choice of venue, but delighted. He would get right into the Silver Fox's lair on their first date. Date? That was hardly the way he should be thinking of Sally. Their first encounter. But he wished it was a date. He liked this Sally Glover, alias Countess someone or other.

"We'd better tell your uncle you're leaving," he said.

"We don't have to do that." She caught Hal's eye and waved, pointing to the door to indicate she was leaving.

John swallowed his disappointment. He noticed Hal looked him up and down very closely, before nodding his consent to Sally's leaving. "Who's the guy your uncle is with?" he asked.

"I have no idea."

He didn't want to arouse her suspicions by insisting on meeting Harmon. Getting into the apartment was too good a lead to lose, so they left.

The minister's limo was still sitting near the door. "Must be some big shot's car," John said leadingly.

"It belongs to the minister of the environment," she said. "He gave the opening speech."

"I'm afraid my car's not that grand. Just a rented job."

"My uncle bought me a convertible. He spoils me," she said fondly. "Of course it didn't come without strings."

John jerked to attention. "Oh?"

"I work for him."

"Oh yes. What do you do?" he asked, listening with both ears.

"He calls me his secretary, but I'm more than that."

"What else do you do?" he asked, willing down the annoyance and rampant curiosity.

Hal didn't tell anyone he was Hugo VanAark. He said he didn't want to be pestered by the press, so she had to answer discreetly. "Sort of a girl Friday. My uncle has a big farm, as well as teaching. There's a lot of paperwork."

That still sounded like a secretary to John. They found his car, and she gave him directions to the apartment building nearby.

Chapter Three

Guelph Tower was a tall, modern apartment building, with enough marble and greenery in the lobby to tell John it wasn't cheap. He noticed it had a doorman decked out in a comic opera uniform. They took the elevator to the penthouse.

His eyes opened wide to see a wall full of original oil paintings by names even he recognized, and he didn't consider himself a connoisseur of art. He hated to walk on the beautiful Persian rug under his feet. It looked as if it should be in a museum. Everything in the room smelled of money—the low-slung white plush sofa with a fur rug slung casually over one end, the plants in big Chinese-looking bowls, the high-tech stereo system, the drapes at the window that shone dully in the lamplight.

He blinked and said, "Wow!"

"Pretty snazzy, eh? My uncle does all right for himself."

John made a mental note of that "eh?" which was a hallmark of Canadian speech. "On a professor's salary?" he asked, since that was all he was supposed to know about the man.

"The farm I mentioned is pretty profitable, too. I'll see about the coffee." She was still carrying her purse when she left.

John heard her speak to someone in the kitchen. A maid! He might have known. Countesses don't usually make their own coffee. He took a quick snoop around the room while she was out. Yup, those paintings were the real McCoy—or darned good forgeries. They were done in oil, at least. He could see the lumps of impasto. They were all signed.

He didn't expect to see any letters from sheikhs in plain view. One open door along the hallway showed him a bank of computers and a wall of filing cabinets that no professor or farmer needed.

Before he could investigate, Sally was back. She still carried her little evening bag, which she tossed on the end of the sofa farthest from him. Then she sat down, putting herself between him and the purse.

"The coffee will be ready in a minute," she said. "I asked Mrs. Locum to bring us some of her coffee cake, too. I don't know about you, but drinks always make me ravenous. Maybe you'd rather have a sandwich. There's some ham and Swiss cheese."

I'm babbling! she thought and closed her mouth. She always tended to do this when she was nervous. And being with John McCallum made her nervous. Not that he was haughty or anything. It was just that she liked him, and wanted to make a good impression.

She sensed that he was getting the wrong impression from her uncle's apartment. He was gazing all around, thinking she was some spoiled millionaire or something.

"Coffee cake is fine," he said. Then he looked at the Rouault of an old king and said in a strained voice, "Is that real?"

"Yes, my uncle collected these pieces in Paris shortly after the war when they were a lot cheaper than they are now."

"They must be worth a fortune. Are they safe here?"

"You're not planning to lift them, are you?" she asked lightly. "If you're a cat burglar in disguise, I should warn you there's an alarm system here equal to that of Fort Knox."

"Thanks for the tip," he said, smiling, and duly noted the fact.

"So, what magazine are you covering the conference for, John?" Sally asked, trying to make harmless conversation.

"The Green Magazine," he answered.

"Is that connected to Green Peace?"

"Yes." Oh lord, he was making a botch of this. "That is—no. Not directly connected, although we share the same view."

"That figures. I never heard of any environmental group being *for* pollution." Now why did I say that? It sounds smart-allecky! "Do you write for other publications as well? I mean since you said you weren't an environment specialist, I assume this isn't your only field."

She was too sharp to suit him! "I'm a free-lance writer. Politics is my field," he said. "I'll be covering the political implications of this conference."

The arrival of the coffee and coffee cake was a welcome diversion. He noticed that Sally had a healthy appetite, despite her small figure. She demolished one piece and was trying to serve him another before he had quite finished.

She was afraid she was making a pig of herself. "Why don't I put on some music?" she said, to give him time to catch up with her.

"That'd be great."

While she was busy at the stereo, he slid along the sofa and nudged her purse open. He nearly choked when he saw the snub-nosed, pearl-handled pistol. He nudged aside her white gloves. Nestling beside them was a blue plastic egg of the sort Silly Putty came in. He stared in disbelief. Silly Putty? His hand went into the purse and palmed the egg. He'd have it analyzed to see what was in it. The weight told him it wasn't empty. He had just closed the evening bag and was about to slide back to the other end of the sofa when she turned around. Did she see him touching her bag? No, she didn't look suspicious.

"What do you like? I have mostly rock, but my uncle has all the boring, classical stuff."

"You choose. Choose Van Halen if you have any. I love his guitar work."

A spontaneous smile lighted her face. "Good choice! I love Van Halen. I don't get to play it much. My uncle calls it 'that infernal racket,'" she said, imitating Hal's voice.

"You seem very close to your uncle."

"I guess since my parents moved out west he's become kind of a surrogate father."

She sat and took another piece of cake. With Van Halen playing noisily in the background, John asked about her life, and she was soon telling him about her studies and her parents. And John found himself believing every word. She seemed like a school teacher's daughter. There was that little streak of defiance that often turned up in the children of ministers and school teachers. They had to prove they were just like the other kids, and sometimes went overboard, using a little too much slang, being ultra casual, in an effort to seem cool.

"How about you, John?" she asked.

John always told the truth when possible. It left fewer things to have to remember. "A New Englander," he said. "My dad ran a sort of department store in a small town, which, I suppose, is why I craved a more dangerous life."

"Dangerous?" she asked at once. "What's so dangerous about writing magazine articles?"

He was furious with himself. How had he let his guard slip like that? It was those darned green eyes, and that smattering of freckles.

He gave a sheepish smile. "I guess that was the wrong word. More interesting is what I meant. My mom thought the city was pretty dangerous."

"Do you live in New York now?" she asked, with bright interest.

"Yeah," he said, as that gave at least some reason for having used the foolish word, dangerous.

"I like a smaller city. Guelph suits me just fine. All my friends are here, and if I want to visit a big city—

you know, to see a live concert or something—Toronto's less than an hour away.''

Was this the talk of a dangerous European countess, an international spy? ''How about your uncle?'' he said, reluctantly bringing the conversation back to business.

''He's semi-retired now. He prefers the quiet life, too.''

''What is he retired from?''

For the first time that evening, John felt he had upset her. She just looked at him for a minute, then said quickly, ''Business. He was a businessman. A representative of a chemical firm. He traveled a lot.''

''I see.'' She was one lousy liar! Her cheeks were pink.

They heard the sound of a key in the lock. ''That'll be him now,'' she said, and dashed into the hallway to meet him. Why did she do that? Presumably he could find his own way in. Was she going to warn him there was company in the house, or maybe inform him he used to be a traveling salesman? John listened sharply to hear how they greeted each other.

''You're home early, Countess,'' a cultured voice said.

Countess! There it was again. He heard a low murmur—was she warning him she had company? Footsteps moved toward the living room.

''You're early too, Hal. No luck?'' she asked.

''That depends on what you call luck. Turn down that infernal racket, will you?''

They came into the room, and John found himself as tongue-tied as a teenager on his first date. The Silver Fox! He was going to meet the Silver Fox! Nothing he had ever imagined did justice to reality. He was so smooth, so handsome, so damned sophisticated. He had stage presence, a bigger-than-life quality that filled the room. John rose automatically to his feet, unaware that Sally was turning off the music.

Then she joined them and said, "Hal, this is John McCallum. He's from the States. John, this is my uncle, Hal Harmon."

Hal gave his hand a firm shake. "Mr. McCallum, delighted to meet you."

"The pleasure is mine, sir. Sally has told me a lot about you." John noticed the Fox was using his own name. But then it was such a well-guarded secret that only the top CIA executive knew it.

Hal put his head back and laughed. "The appalling girl! Can you not find something interesting to talk about, Sal? Really, boring your young man with tales of your poor old uncle. And serving him coffee! Let me make you a drink, Mr. McCallum."

John said, "Please—"

"There, you see," Hal said chidingly to Sally. "The man is perishing for a drink."

"I meant please call me John, sir."

The Silver Fox smiled benignly at the fine impression he was giving. "What's your poison, John?"

"Well, uh, whatever you're having, sir."

Hal tilted his head and smiled. "I haven't been knighted during my absence, have I, Sal? All these 'sir's!' are going to my head. My name's Hal. I'm having a Scotch."

"That'll be fine," John said, smiling in spite of himself. He was having a drink with the Silver Fox! He could hardly wait to tell his colleagues. Every atom of his being wanted to sit at the legend's feet and hear stories of his illustrious career.

"I hope you don't mind a single malt. I acquired the taste for it when I was in Scotland." Hal made the drinks at a small cocktail table as he talked. "And a disgusting, sweet, sticky Irish Cream for you, Sal. I'm trying to educate my niece's palate, but she is strangely immune to quality. Prefers hamburgers to steak, has an inexplicable fondness for blue jeans and tells me she didn't much like Paris. Too many Frenchmen—and her major at college was French. I ask you!"

Hal handed them their drinks but didn't sit down. He tossed off his own drink quickly and said, "I shan't interrupt your little tête-à-tête. I'll be in my office if you need me, Sal. I have a few calls to make. Nice meeting you, John." He left, murmuring to himself, "Let me see, what time is it in Vienna?" He disappeared into the computer room and closed the door behind him.

When John returned to earth, he found Sally gazing at him with a curious look on her face. "You seemed nervous of Hal," she said in a questioning way.

"Did I? He's very interesting," he said lamely.

"Yeah, I know what you mean. He kind of takes over a room. You don't have to drink that rotgut if you don't like it. Bad as plain Scotch is, a single malt is worse."

"This is the best money can buy," he said. But legend or not, John didn't care for his brand of Scotch.

Conversation was strangely stilted once Hal left them. John was acutely aware that the Silver Fox was just feet away, behind that closed door, probably with his ear to the keyhole. What would happen when he left? Would Sally join him? Would there be a jealous scene, with Hal demanding to know why she had brought a man home? It no longer seemed odd that she should be in love with a man old enough to be her father. The Silver Fox was ageless, timeless, charming, overwhelming. What stories he could tell, if only John could get him to admit who he was.

But he was here to do a job, and it was time to get on with it. He'd go back to the conference party before it was over and try to identify the man Hal had been talking to. Get that Silly Putty egg analyzed, check the fingerprints on it, if there were any.

He also wanted to firm up his relationship with Sally, because he planned to get back into the apartment when the Fox was away and search his office. A bug on the telephone would help.

"This has been really nice, Sally," he said, setting aside his glass. Water droplets had gathered on the outside. He used them as an excuse to wipe his prints off. He'd already taken care of his coffee cup and fork. He hadn't touched anything else, had he? Maybe he was being overly cautious, but there was no point taking chances with the Silver Fox.

"You know where I live," she said, with a friendly smile. "If you have any time free from the conference, give me a buzz. I'll show you the town."

"When are you free?" he asked.

"I can pretty much make my own hours. I work here, at home."

Perfect! "Then I'll call you tomorrow. Maybe we can do lunch."

"Sounds good. Where are you staying, in case I want to get in touch with you?"

After just a moment's pause he said, "The College Inn."

"That's a nice place, and it's handy to the convention."

"Yeah. Well, it's been fun." He rose and took one last look around at the Fox's lair. They'd all be dying to hear about it back in Washington. They didn't know about the art collection, for instance. The sly old fox was certainly getting a lot of money from somewhere.

"I'll go to the door with you," Sally said, and got up to accompany him.

He hesitated a moment at the open door, wondering if he should kiss her goodnight. He towered a foot above her. Funny how he always seemed to prefer small women, when he was over six feet himself. In the darkened hallway, her hair lost its glow. It looked nearly black, in stark contrast to her pale skin, with the smattering of freckles. He liked freckles, too, especially when they were spread across such a cute little nose. The dangly earrings gave her the air of a girl dressing up in her mom's clothes and jewelry.

She gave an encouraging smile, and he reached for her. The raw silk of her dress felt cool beneath his fingers. Her flesh was firmly muscled. He could span her waist with his two hands, with an inch left over. He placed a small kiss at the corner of her lips. His jaw brushed her curls, releasing a light flowery scent that just suited her, more like herbal shampoo than perfume.

When he stepped back to leave, she was gazing at him, with eyes that looked dark in the shadows. It was impossible to tell from her expression what she was thinking. Then a small smile lifted her lips, and she said, "Good night, John."

"See you soon," he said, and left.

He should be feeling triumphant. The case was going well. He had made contact, met the Fox, got into his house and had a date to meet the Countess tomorrow. So why did he feel as if he wanted to quit his job? He had never met anyone just like Sally before. The women encountered in his line of work tended to be older, more world-weary. He wanted to take Sally home and put her behind a white picket fence. She'd probably hate it, but she didn't belong in the sordid world of espionage, either.

But that's where she was—right smack in the middle of his case, threatening to ruin his concentration and his career. Because if he blew this case—well, he just couldn't, that's all. He returned to the party. The man Hal had been speaking with was just leaving, but John managed to meet him. He was Aswar Ranji, an environmentalist from Kuwait. Funny he wasn't using an alias, either. Ranji was on the panel that was going to discuss capping the wells in his country. John avoided mentioning the name Hal Harmon to Ranji. He'd let Washington know Ranji was here. He'd also notify the RCMP, in case they weren't on to him. Staynor had arranged for him to work with the Mounties. They could analyze the Silly Putty and check Sally's fingerprints. Since she was so anxious to hide them, they must be on file.

As soon as Hal heard the front door close, he came out of the computer room.

"Why did you go in there, Hal?" Sally asked. "You hate computers. Where you eavesdropping on my date?"

"Yes. Is he gone?" he asked sharply.

"He just left. Why?"

"Because he's up to no good, that's why."

"It's not you he's interested in. It's me," she said with a cocky look. "We're having lunch tomorrow."

"The hell you are! He's up to something."

"You're paranoid. He's just a journalist from the States."

"Then why did he follow you out of the hall when you went to plant the bomb? Did that go all right, by the way?"

"It went fine. What do you mean, he followed me?"

"He followed you from the minute we arrived. And he kept a damned sharp eye on me as well. I bet he's gone back to that conference to get a line on Ranji. He was at your shoulder when you spoke to the minister of the environment. He followed you out and came back a minute behind you. Then he accosted you at the bar."

"Why didn't you warn me?"

"You should have kept an eye over your shoulder. I followed you when you left the party with him. Once I saw he was bringing you home, I knew you were safe, for tonight at least. He didn't get into my office?"

"Of course not," she said angrily. Her anger was directed at John, but since he had left, she had to take it out on Hal. "What do you think he's up to anyway?"

"He's from Wigo, of course."

"Oh!" Sally said, and laughed. "I was afraid you thought he was a spy or something."

"He is a spy—for Wigo publishing. They're trying to find out what project I'm working on and beat me to the punch. Writing inferior parodies of my works isn't enough for them. They want to see what I have in the offing and plagiarize it. Don't laugh! There's big money in this sort of fiction. Who did he say he worked for?''

"Green Magazine."

"I never heard of it. I'll check my directory."

He disappeared into the office. Sally just relaxed against the luxurious fur rug on the sofa. Funny John hadn't given her the gears about using real fur. Any environmentalist worth his salt would have been against it. But he wasn't a specialist in that area. It was strange *Green Magazine* would have sent someone who *wasn't* a specialist to the conference.... She shook the thought away.

John was nice—honest and open. Her uncle had a persecution complex where his writing was concerned. Nobody was trying to rip him off.

Hal returned, his face flushed with annoyance. "There's no such publication as *Green Magazine*. I told you he was from Wigo. I'm going to call Ranji and warn him not to speak to McCallum. Ranji knows exactly what *After the Storm* is all about. He was my main source of up-to-the-minute background, since he was in the East at the time."

Sally still wasn't convinced that Hal was right. But when he returned a minute later and gave his report, she began to have second thoughts.

Hal said, "I got hold of Ranji just as he entered his room at the hotel. McCallum did go back to the party and made a point of meeting Ranji. That was no co-incidence."

"It looks like you're right," she admitted.

"I'll check his fingerprints," Hal said. "If Wigo has hired a private eye, his prints will be on record with the FBI. The local fuzz will help me out there. We enjoy good relations. I bought a thousand dollars' worth of tickets to their ball.''

Sally listened in disillusionment. She had really liked John, and she thought he liked her, too. Something had seemed to spark between them. But if her uncle was right, he didn't care a hoot about her. He was just using her.

"I'll tell him I'm busy when he calls tomorrow—if he calls," she said.

"On the contrary! You must go out with him. Find out where he's staying. We'll have to get into his room."

"He's staying at the College Inn. Most of the delegates are."

"I'll check with the convention secretary and see if they know anything about him." A slow grin spread over Hal's face. "I'm rather enjoying this. It's like old times, being back in the game. A pity I hadn't a more worthwhile opponent than young McCallum. I'll settle his hash in less than twenty-four hours. Which is his glass?"

Sally pointed it out. Hal carefully lifted it with his handkerchief. As an afterthought, he took his coffee cup and plate and fork as well.

When he noticed Sally was looking glum, he said, "No long faces, my dear. You haven't had time to fall in love with McCallum yet. This will be a chance to try your skills on a real case."

"Yes, but spying wasn't the skill I hoped to try on John."

"There are plenty of fish in the sea, Sal. I'll take you to Europe when the book is finished and introduce you to some eligible men. I know a young viscount...."

Sally just shook her head. "What would I have in common with a viscount, for crying out loud?"

"By the time I've finished polishing your social graces, you'll be fit for a duke."

"I don't want a duke, Hal. I just want some nice guy like John McCallum. Oh well, like you said, there are plenty of fish in the sea. Too bad the good ones always get away. Good night."

She emptied her evening bag before retiring. She smiled at the toy gun and white gloves, dusty now from her night's work. She tossed them into the laundry hamper, then frowned at the little pile of stuff from her purse. Lipstick, tiny brush, ten dollars, in case she had to take a cab, her keys, some paper tissues. Something was missing....

The Silly Putty! She remembered putting it back in her purse. What could have happened to it? She also remembered John moving away from her purse when she came back from the stereo. He had looked a little funny.

Had he searched her purse? He would have seen the gun—but why on earth would he steal her Silly Putty? It didn't make any sense. She must have dropped it before she closed her purse, when she was at the minister's car. She undressed and went to bed, thinking of John. He had such nice eyes, a deep blue, with long lashes. And he was probably a spy for Wigo. Too bad.

Chapter Four

John sat in his room, tossing the egg of Silly Putty into the air. The RCMP had given it back with their report. The Silly Putty was just that—Silly Putty. And the egg was on his face.

"If you've got any dangerous marbles or baseballs you'd like us to analyze, don't hesitate to bring them in, Mr. McCallum," the Mountie had said with a smirk. "Always glad to lend a hand. I didn't realize the CIA were making copies of the comic strips. That's about all Silly Putty's good for."

They had no record of prints for Sally Glover, so at least she wasn't a known criminal. A Sally Glover *had* attended Lester B. Pearson High School. She was the daughter of Margaret Glover (née Harmon), and Ronald James Glover, formerly a teacher at Guelph High School, now retired to Victoria, British Columbia. That checked out all right.

Such a person did exist. If Sally was that person, then her mother was the Silver Fox's sister. John hoped that was the relationship between them—uncle and niece. But why did Harmon call her Countess? The Mounties were still following that one up for him.

It was beginning to look as if the sly old fox had recruited Sally, either by money or blackmail. He might have some hold over her. Her father had retired early, the report didn't give a reason. A criminal father, maybe, or even some petty crime she'd committed herself? Shoplifting, for instance? Or maybe he'd just played on her sense of adventure, getting her to believe he was still working for the CIA?

John canvased the possible ways of spending his afternoon. Ranji's panel discussion on the Kuwait disaster—he'd check in to see that Harmon was there, which would mean he wasn't at his apartment. Not much hope of getting in, with that Fort Knox security system and a live-in maid on the premises. Unless he could get Sally to invite him....

He phoned her from his hotel room to confirm their luncheon date. He thought she sounded a little stiff. Was she on to him? No, she couldn't be yet. In any case, she agreed to lunch.

"Where do you suggest?" he asked.

"Why don't I meet you at your hotel? They have a nice dining room."

"I'll pick you up," he said.

"You don't have to do that, John. I'll meet you there."

He didn't want to betray his eagerness to get into the apartment and said, "Fine. Say, twelvish, in the lobby?"

"Or I can meet you at your room," she countered.

"If I'm not in the lobby, then you come on up."

"What room is it?" she asked. Again he sensed that strained note in her voice.

"Room 203." He'd be sure to be waiting in the lobby. He didn't trust her eagerness to get into his room. If all she wanted was privacy for romance, it'd be different, but he didn't think Sally, the demure Sally he'd seen, meant that. He should have insisted on picking her up. Driving her own car meant she'd drive herself home, leaving him no excuse to get back into the apartment. He was afraid that was exactly why she'd insisted.

"I'll see you there," she said, and hung up.

In the apartment, Sally turned to her uncle. "It's all set. He's in room 203, and he was reluctant to let me meet him there."

"Find out if he's going to the lecture this afternoon. That'll leave you a couple of hours to get in and do a search."

"How do I get in?"

"The same way you got into my room without a key in Toronto, for *Before the Storm*. This isn't like you to be so dim-witted, Sally. I hope you're not falling for this fellow. That's the mark of a rank amateur."

"Of course not," she scowled.

"Be sure to tell him I'm attending the conference. That'll ensure his attendance."

"Okay, but if you're wrong, Hal, I'll expect an apology."

"Wrong? How can I be wrong? There is no *Green Magazine*. He made a beeline for Ranji as soon as he left here last night. He's sticking to you like Velcro, and he didn't leave a single print on anything he touched in this apartment. The police said everything had been wiped clean. If he's innocent, I'll eat my shirt."

"You're right," she admitted reluctantly. "The lack of prints pretty well clinches it. I'll try to get a set at lunch."

"He'll be on his guard," Hal cautioned. "I suggest you take that big black patent leather purse. Wipe it clean before you go, and drop it at his feet. He'll have to pick it up for you."

"I remember all Sophia's tricks, Hal. You don't have to coach me."

"There'll be a handsome bonus in it for you—a little holiday. I know your fondness for Italy. I'll give you some letters of introduction. The Conte d'Albergesia is an old friend."

"How old?" she asked, with more doubt than interest.

"Seventy-ish, but his son is young—forty something."

"That young? Gee, I don't know if I want to rob the cradle. Does the son have a son?"

"I keep forgetting you're such a child. Never mind. You'll meet Mr. Right one of these days, and I shall lose you," he said with a sigh.

"I'm a woman now, Hal."

"You'll always be little Sally to me. I remember dandling you on my knee. You used to call me Unca Hal. Your father was so proud of you."

She saw through all his tricks. Now he was using this emotional blackmail to make sure she did as he wanted. It really wasn't necessary. If John was working for Wigo, she'd be only too happy to expose him. Stealing her uncle's work was despicable.

"I'll take my beeper to the lecture. Give me a buzz as soon as you're out of his room," Hal said. "That'll be the signal I can leave. I bet McCallum leaves on my heels. You and I will meet back here."

"Okay. I'm going to get ready for lunch now. What do you expect me to find in his room?"

"Anything that suggests he's working for Wigo. He might have a picture of me, or my address jotted down, or instructions from his agency. A phone number. Anything."

Sally went to her room to change for her date. She liked the new suits with split skirts. They looked dressy but felt casual. Her favorite was a wildly patterned top in black and yellow and red and green, with a plain green skirt to tone it down. The black patent bag would go well with it, too. Her earrings, a jangle of colored beads, matched the suit. She wiped the bag clean of prints with a damp facecloth, and was ready to go. It was such a beautiful day she put the top of her car down to enjoy the fresh air and sun.

John was waiting for her in the lobby of the College Inn, to make sure she didn't get into his room. He looked even better than last night. The formal attire hadn't suited him. He was an outdoors, athletic type. He'd look more at home on a baseball field, or on horseback.

His spontaneous smile was so natural that she thought for a minute there was some gigantic misunderstanding. John was nice, dammit! He was what the boy next door should be like, but never was.

He reached out a finger and playfully flicked her earring. "Don't your ears get tired, carrying all that weight?" he grinned. On impulse, he bent down and kissed her, just a fleeting kiss on the corner of her lips, but his lightest touch made her tingle. Some piney scent lingered around him, from soap or after-shave.

"They're light. Just plastic," she said.

"You're not into diamonds? I thought maybe your uncle—"

"Diamonds aren't worn in the daytime. And let's not talk about him," she said gruffly.

"Sorry I asked."

They went into the dining room.

It was crowded with the convention crew, but John had reserved a table. Everything was fancy, with white tablecloths and red serviettes and a bouquet of flowers, Michaelmas daisies and red carnations.

"Let's start with a drink," he suggested.

"I don't drink so early in the day," Sally said, "but you go ahead." Her look implied he was an alcoholic and should get help fast.

John bit back his temper. This lunch was getting off to a bad start, and it wasn't his fault. "Did you and your uncle have a little tiff?" he asked, through thin lips.

His manner made Sally realize she was being difficult. Since she was going to be with him for an hour or so, there was no point making the lunch worse than it need be.

"We're not going to talk about him, remember?" She smiled, to soften the reproach. "Maybe I will have something to drink. Some wine with lunch." Darn it! She'd forgotten to drop her purse!

They both ordered the fettuccine Alfredo. John ordered a bottle of dry white wine to go with it. She noticed that he sipped his slowly. Was he afraid he'd get tight and say something indiscreet, or was he just showing her his lack of interest in alcohol?

The fettuccine came in a creamy Parmesan sauce with a pungent under-taste of garlic and little bits of ham. They helped themselves to house salad from the buffet. They were both eager to establish a friendlier mood and used the food as a safe bridge for conversation.

"I guess you'll be covering the Kuwait lecture for your magazine this afternoon, eh?" she said. "I mean since it's the highlight of the whole convention."

That unconscious "eh?" reinforced the notion that she was a Canadian and not a shady countess.

"I can't miss that, but I could cut out early," he said. "You're not going?" What he wanted to ask was if her uncle was attending.

"No, but my uncle is." There, she'd told him, and now they could really forget Hal.

"I thought he wasn't much interested in the conference."

"That's the only lecture he does plan to attend—just for general information."

"What did you say he taught at the college?"

"Marketing," she said briefly, and filled her fork with pasta.

"Is that his background? You mentioned something about a farm...."

"That's just a hobby. He has a business background. Didn't I tell you last night he was a chemical salesman?" she said. She remembered it only too well. "His dad was a farmer, though. That's why he bought Hilltop Farm. It's a really neat old-fashioned house, and of course it has barns and a silo. He has a hundred cows, but it's the horses I really like."

"You ride!" he exclaimed, with a joyous smile.

"I love it. He bought me my own horse, Fandango. She's a thoroughbred—well, part thoroughbred.'"

"Sounds like a contradiction in terms to me!" John laughed. "I never rode a thoroughbred but my uncle had a farm back in New England. I used to ride this old cob, Buck. Boy, did he buck! You needed Crazy Glue to stay on his back."

Sally had gone to lunch with every intention of being stiff and standoffish and not liking John. But when they began exchanging riding stories, she forgot all about it. Riders are worse than fishermen for their tall tales. For every tumble she had taken, John had a story to outdo her. Buck had bitten him and stepped on his foot—on purpose—breaking three toes. But the worst crime was when he had dumped John into a manure pile in front of his friends.

"Funny how we go on liking them so much, when they treat us like dirt," she said. "It's a very strange relationship between horses and people. You don't find dogs acting like that. My Shep is faithful to a fault. He doesn't leave my heels when I'm at the farm. No matter how long I've been away, he comes dashing out to meet me, tail wagging."

"You have a dog!" John exclaimed. "I have one at home. Max is half Lab, half mongrel. Stupid as the day is long. He eats my Mom's cactus plants. You'd think he'd learn. I spent an hour trying to pick the needles out of his mouth, with him squirming and howling. The next day, he was right back at it again. A glutton for punishment."

"Shep eats corn on the cob," she announced in an effort to top him. "He gets it on the ground between his paws and gnaws the cob as clean as a whistle. There

isn't a shred of a kernel left when he's finished with it.
I wish you could see Shep.''

"I wouldn't say no if you invited me to Hilltop," he
replied, and beamed a hundred-watt smile at her.

She had to bite back the instinctive urge to invite
him. She noticed he'd missed one corner of his jaw
when he had shaved. A patch of whiskers about the
size of a dime cast a shadow. For some reason, it
touched her deeply. It made him seem so boyish. Hal
would never leave the house with a single one showing.

"What do you say?" he prodded, when she didn't
answer.

She felt a warm tide rise up in her embarrassment.
Hal would kill her if she invited John to Hilltop. How
had she let herself slip into this freewheeling conversation? She had forgotten all about John working for
Wigo. He was so easy to talk to, she felt she'd known
him forever. Once in a rare while you meet a person
who seems like the other half of yourself, and that was
exactly the way she felt about John. She almost felt as
if she had known him before, in some previous incar-
nation.

If she had sat and written up a list of qualities she
liked in a man, John would have filled every wish—
except integrity, of course. He wasn't a show-off like
Hal. She liked her uncle in spite of his sophisticated
ways, not because of them. John was so natural and
he seemed genuinely interested in her. At least he
didn't monopolize the conversation. He listened, and
he had the most gorgeous blue eyes she'd ever seen in
her life.

"Too bad you're not staying awhile longer," she
said.

"I'll be here a few days. Maybe we can work in a visit before I leave." Again he looked at her expectantly.

"I'll see when Hal plans to visit the farm," she said, and felt stupid. There was no reason Hal had to go with them.

"Like you said, you're not his Siamese twin."

"He might need me here, is what I meant."

It was time for dessert. When John suggested the pastry tray, she knew she had met her soul mate. They both examined the delightful confections.

"That Black Forest cake looks so good, but the strawberry cheesecake runs it a close second," Sally said, her eyes devouring both.

"Decisions, decisions. Let's go for broke and have both."

"I couldn't! I'll burst my seams. I'll have the Black Forest cake, you have the cheesecake, and we'll split, like a Chinese dinner."

"You've got a deal."

Sally lined both plates up in the middle of the table and they attacked the desserts vigorously. There was very little conversation while they were reveling in the voluptuous charms of whipped cream and cherries and chocolate. When the plates were empty, they sat back and tasted their coffee.

"I think the cheesecake won," John said. "The Black Forest tasted a little bitter after it."

"That's because you ate them in the wrong order. If you'd eaten the Black Forest cake first, they would both have tasted perfect. That's the advice of an expert dessert eater. Save the sweetest until the last."

"I bow to your superior knowledge. We eat and learn. When's the next time you can share a pastry tray with me? Dinner tonight?"

She smiled shyly, happy that he wanted to see her again, even if it might not be possible. "I'll have to check with Hal, see what he has on."

"I'm glad he pays you so well, since he seems to have first dibs on your evenings, as well as your days." His quizzical look asked for an explanation.

"He pays very well," she said.

The mention of Hal had its usual damping effect on their conversation. They finished their coffee quickly and refused a second cup. Sally remembered to drop her purse when she stood up. She knew then that Hal wasn't just imagining that John was up to dirty tricks. He just stood there, staring at the purse in dismay, without picking it up.

"You dropped your purse," he said.

"I noticed. It's all right, John. I don't carry crystal or anything fragile in it." Since he just left it lying on the floor, she bent over to retrieve it.

"Allow me," John said, and picked it up before she reached it. He carefully looped one finger under the brass chain and handed it to her. Not a chance of getting a print from the chain. "What do you keep in here? Rocks? Bowling balls?" he joked.

"No, I carry them in my other bag. Thanks. Would you like me to drop you off at the conference?"

"It's a bit early. And I still have my rented car. Will I be seeing you again?"

"You know my number," she said with a flirtatious smile, and left, carrying her big black patent bag that took fingerprints so well. John's eyes narrowed in suspicion.

She'd dropped it on purpose. So Hal had either checked his glass for prints last night and found out he'd wiped them off, or he had just turned suspicious. Maybe Ranji had phoned him. He noticed Ranji had left the party right after he had wangled an introduction to him. Either way, John realized he had to be extremely careful.

He watched Sally go, her derriere swinging lightly in counterpoint to the purse. The walk wasn't conscious or exaggerated, but a natural feminine movement that was beautiful to watch. He refused to believe she knew what her uncle was up to, working hand in glove with the enemy.

The Silver Fox would have a pretty good idea of U.S. military strategy. He could give useful advice to Ranji. That Ranji actually was, apparently, an environmentalist from Kuwait meant nothing. Anyone could be a traitor in this modern world. Even the Silver Fox.

But that didn't mean Sally knew. The Fox must have fed her some story. He'd probably convinced her that he, John, was a bad guy. Sally was certainly suspicious of him, but underneath it all, she liked him. A man could sense a thing like that. There was a strong physical attraction, and more important, a meeting of minds.

John hadn't the least enthusiasm for the job of catching his old hero. It would hurt him nearly as much as it hurt Sally. And it wouldn't be easy, either. Harmon had never even come close to being caught by the most clever foreign agents when he was in the field. He foresaw every move, and he took steps to avoid capture. Did he know CIA were on to him, or was he always this careful of strangers, checking up on them?

John knew he would have to tread very carefully. Seeing Sally seemed the ploy most likely to keep an eye on the Fox, and for once his professional judgment concurred with personal preference. He'd try to discover just how much Sally knew and, if possible, protect her when her uncle was arrested.

From the door of the hotel he saw Sally leaving the parking lot. She was driving a little red convertible, the one her generous uncle had given her. Her red hair gleamed like a new penny in the sun. She took the turn that led to Hal's apartment. John figured she was going home to make her report. Well, she hadn't found out much—except that he wasn't eager to show his fingerprints. It didn't really matter. They weren't officially on file anywhere except at CIA, but the Fox might have someone working for him there. Anything was possible.

Sally drove home and dumped her purse on the table. "It didn't work," she announced. "No prints. He picked the darned thing up by the chain."

"That, in itself, is as good as an admission of guilt," Hal said. "Is he attending the lecture this afternoon?"

"Yes, and I told him you'd be there."

"Excellent. It starts at two-thirty. Be sure you ask the hotel desk to phone his room before you try to get it. It would be embarrassing if you walked in on him."

"Sure, Hal, and I'll remember to wipe my nose next time I sneeze, too."

"A trifle miffed, are we?" he asked, lifting an eyebrow.

"He was hinting pretty strongly to get to Hilltop. Why would he want to do that?"

"He has no way of knowing where Hugo VanAark does his writing. But since I do it here, there's no harm in letting him waste his time at Hilltop, if you're enjoying your little game of cat and mouse. In fact, it would keep him out of mischief while I finish up the last few chapters here. And it would be good practice for you, Sal. The Countess would have got prints. You could have snitched a fork from the table."

"Yes, and he would have snitched it back before I left. He's not exactly an amateur, you know. So, do you want me to go alone with him to the farm?" she asked, trying to conceal her excitement.

"You wouldn't be alone. The Hudsons are there."

Mr. Hudson ran the farm, and his wife was the housekeeper cum receptionist. The farm got plenty of business calls.

"We'll see," Sally said. "John asked me out tonight. No particular reason I shouldn't go, is there? I might manage to snag his prints."

"I'll need you here. I'm having a little party. With the environment looming so large on the horizon, it's time I learned more about it. It's a plot possibility for the future. The crowd gathered for the conference are all experts. It's too good an opportunity to miss. You're looking glum, Countess," he said playfully. "You can invite your John to the party if you like. I'll make sure to lock my office door—and check my phone for bugs when he leaves."

She looked at the phone in alarm. Hal shook his head. "No, he hasn't gotten around to it yet. Rather remiss of him, but then a bugged phone has to be monitored, and I believe he's working alone. Wigo is a cheap outfit," he said with a cluck of his tongue. "I should think Hugo VanAark merits at least a pair of spies."

"Doesn't your neck get tired, lugging that big head around?" she asked with a bold grin.

"No, my dear. My head grew gradually, along with my bank account, and my neck seems to have acquired the strength to carry it. It's time to leave for the conference. I—and my large head—will see you later."

"Sorry about that crack, Hal. I'll head back to the hotel, with gloves," she said, and left.

She drove around until two-thirty, then she went to the hotel parking lot. When she didn't see John's rented car, she placed a call to his room from the front desk. She let the phone ring seven times, then hung up. She went upstairs, found room 203, and tapped on the door. No answer. There was a hotel maid across the hall, preparing a vacant room.

Sally went to her and said, "I've forgotten my key. Could you let me into room 203?"

The cleaning woman looked at her uncertainly. Sally drew a small bill out of her purse. "The room's registered under the name McCallum, if you want to phone the desk and check," she said, nodding to the phone.

The woman shrugged her shoulders, took the money and unlocked the door for her. It always amazed Sally that it was so easy to get into a person's hotel room. It seemed to her the desk would hand over the key to anyone, if she knew the name and room number, and was well dressed. And if the desk wouldn't, the maid usually would.

Once she was inside, she put on her gloves and headed straight for the tan suitcase on the luggage bench at the end of the bed. It was closed but not locked. She lifted it up and knew it was too heavy for a supposedly empty suitcase. There was nothing visible inside at a glance. No papers, no pictures of Hal or anyone else. She tried the bottom with her fingertips. It seemed solid, but she soon heard the rasp of velcro being pulled loose. She lifted up the false bottom and stared at an assortment of electronic gizmos, each fitted into a sponge tray, held with elastic grips.

So Hal was right, damn his eyes. John *was* a spy. It wasn't fair for a spy to love horses and dogs and rich desserts. They should be lean and mean, like Hal. She wrenched her attention back to the job. She recognized some listening devices of various sorts, but soon her fingers moved to a larger item, wrapped in a flannelette shoe-polishing cloth. It was roughly the shape of a gun.

She pulled out the bundle and unwrapped it. It was a small pistol. She released the cartridge and saw it held bullets. Boy, Wigo wasn't fooling around! How did John get this through customs? Maybe a P.I. was allowed to bring a gun into the country. She rewrapped the gun, returned it to the sponge protector, pushed the false bottom back in place and closed the suitcase.

She took a quick peek around the rest of the room. The only literature she found had to do with the conference. John hadn't circled any particular lectures or the names of any participants. It seemed fairly innocent. She went into the bathroom. Just toilet supplies in a black bag. The clothes closet held his black jacket and some shirts on the top shelf. There was nothing in the jacket pockets. Not so much as a comb or a candy bar.

She went to check the pad by the phone. He might have jotted down a name or phone number. Maybe Wigo's phone number, for instance. The pad was bare. There was no indented impression on the top page, where a pen had left its trace of a number torn off. Fingerprints! This was her chance to take something with his prints on it. Something he wouldn't miss right away. The maid had cleaned the room. The glasses were wrapped in a paper protector.

She looked around, then ran back into the bathroom. She rooted through the contents of the black case; shaving cream and after-shave lotion and toothpaste. He might have left a print on them, but of course he'd miss them and have a pretty good idea who had taken them. She hesitated, lifting one after another, peering for prints.

Hidden beneath them she saw a little blue egg of Silly Putty. The one that had suddenly disappeared from her purse last night. John had taken it. What on earth for? It was a good surface for holding prints. She held it up to the light. Was that smudge a fingerprint? It wasn't hers, because she had worn gloves when she handled it. She slipped it into her purse and went back into the bedroom.

When she heard the rattle of the key in the lock, she assumed it was the maid, probably having second thoughts about letting her in. They were getting a little better about security. She quickly peeled off her gloves and composed a nonchalant face as the door opened. John McCallum stepped in.

"John!" One loud, horrified exclamation escaped before she recovered her cool. It was time to become Countess Sophia. The Countess had weathered worse ordeals than this.

"Sally! What are you doing here?" he demanded, but he seemed more perplexed than angry.

She hunched her shoulders and plopped playfully on the bed. "Waiting for you to come back," she said. "I knew you wouldn't stay all afternoon at that dull lecture. You got a copy of Ranji's speech, right?"

"Yes, as a matter of fact, I did." *And I also saw that Harmon was there, and thought this was my chance to call you and get into his apartment.* His eyes moved warily around the room. The suitcase wasn't open. He didn't have anything else to worry about— did he? "How did you get in?" he asked.

"The maid let me in."

"Why didn't you phone?" he asked, setting down his briefcase.

"I wanted to surprise you." She could see he wasn't quite buying that, so she rattled on. "Besides, I wanted to leave you a note. Hal's having a party tonight. We'd like you to come." She waited for the next question. *Why didn't you leave the note at the desk?*

"He invited me?" John exclaimed.

"I'm inviting you. It's all right. I told him I was."

While they were talking, the phone rang, and John picked it up. Sally sat with her nerves screaming. She had a strong feeling it was Hal, phoning to warn her that John had left the lecture early.

"McCallum here," John said. He listened, frowning, then said again, "Hello. McCallum here. Hello." He set the phone down. "Nobody there. It must have been a wrong number."

Sally was certain then that it had been Hal on the other end of the line. He'd be worried sick about her. And his next move would be to come storming over to

John's room to rescue her. That would really make John suspicious.

"Shall we go?" she said, jumping up off the bed.

John sensed her nervousness and began to wonder about that phone call. He soon figured out it was Harmon, phoning Sally to warn her. He wanted time to figure out his next move, since they were on to him. He also wanted to go over his room with a fine-tooth comb and see just what was missing. He didn't think he'd left anything incriminating around. The pictures of Hal and Sally were in his jacket pocket, along with his briefing notes.

"I'd really love to, Sally," he said, "but I'm just a working stiff. I should get busy on this story if I'm going to that party tonight." Her sigh of relief wasn't audible, but it was visible. Her face relaxed noticeably.

"Gee, that's too bad. But you will come tonight?" she asked, to give an air of eagerness to her pursuit of him.

"I'd love to. Will it be a big party?" Hopefully big enough to allow me to roam a bit, unobserved.

"Probably. Hal's inviting some delegates from the convention. You might learn some interesting things for your article."

"Kill two birds with one stone." He smiled. "What time?"

"Nine-ish. It isn't formal, but I wouldn't wear jeans, either, if you know what I mean."

"I'll be looking forward to it."

"See you then."

He accompanied her to the door. They stopped and looked at each other. John saw the shadow of fear in her eyes and felt an urge to rescue her from this life of crime.

He took her two hands and said, "Sally, if there's anything I can do for you—anything—let me know." His voice fell to a hush, but she heard the sincerity, and the worry, in it. He drew her closer, until their bodies were just touching. "You can trust me, sweetheart."

Caught off guard by the sudden change in mood, Sally just gazed from her tilted green eyes. Sweetheart! He had called her sweetheart. A dreamy look came over her. She noticed he still hadn't shaved off that patch of whiskers. At this close range, she could see each individual hair. She could also smell his after-shave—a sort of pine-and-cinnamon smell. She wanted to feel that little patch of whiskers against her smooth skin. It would be rough, exciting.

Her face lifted involuntarily to his. As if caught in a magnetic force, his lowered to hers. Their lips touched, and an involuntary shiver seized her. She could almost swear a real, physical electric spark flashed between them when that little patch of whiskers prickled her cheek. It was soon forgotten in the tumult of other sensations. Their lips clung, and slowly, like the inevitable force of a peach ripening in the warmth of the sun, the kiss deepened to passion.

His arms closed around her possessively, until she could feel the compelling masculine heat of his body warming hers.

His muscles were taut and hard against her. This was all wrong. She shouldn't let him— Then a moist flicker eased her lips open, and she gave up the struggle. She knew she was lost when his tongue began its masterful caressing tactics, mating with hers, then darting off on further explorations—brushing, tantalizing, encouraging. His hands pushed her blouse aside and moved over the tender sides of her body with roughly gentle strokes.

A hot flood of pleasure rushed through her, driving her onward. She had to rise on tiptoe to get both her arms firmly around his neck. His hair felt rough and prickly like dry corn silk as she drove her fingers through it, luxuriating in the intimacy. His arms lowered, gathering her hips against him and moving her in slow, sensual circles that caused a pounding assault in her head and heart. She felt hot and suffocated, and she never wanted it to stop.

They didn't even hear the bellboy coming along the hall, until he uttered a discreet little cough. He gave a knowing smile and said, "Sorry to interrupt you, sir, but this message came for you at the desk. The gentleman said your phone didn't seem to be working and asked me to deliver it personally. Urgent, he said."

Sally smiled softly to see John was as embarrassed as she was at being caught in that hot embrace. It told her that whatever his other sins, he wasn't a hardened womanizer.

"Thanks," John said, and handed the bellboy a loonie. Then he frowned at it and handed him another.

The boy said, "Thank you, sir," and left.

"Was that enough?" John asked.

"Of course it was. Those loonies are a buck."

"I'm used to paper dollars. Why do they call it a loonie?"

"Because it has a loon on the back. That funny-looking bird."

"Oh, I thought it was supposed to be a duck."

He opened the note and read it. It was an invitation from Hal to the party that night. The old devil had phoned his room and hung up so his voice wouldn't be recognized. He was afraid Sally had been caught red-handed and sent the bellboy up with this "urgent" note to make sure she didn't come to any harm. At least he was taking some precautions for Sal's safety.

"It's from your uncle," he said, "inviting me to tonight's party."

"I guess he was afraid I wouldn't get in touch with you."

"Two invitations. Now I'll be sure to be there."

"You better come twice," she said, and laughed nervously.

After an awkward moment of silence, Sally said, "What did you mean, John, about if I need help?"

"Just what I said. If your uncle is, uh, persuading you to do anything you don't like, you can count on my help. All the way."

"Thanks," she said, "but Hal isn't as overbearing as you think. I'm not overworked. You'll see, when you get to know him."

She stopped and asked herself why she was apologizing for her uncle. Hal wasn't doing anything wrong. It was John who should be apologizing. Maybe she should be trying to save John.

"Listen, John," she said on impulse, "is there anything you want to tell me? You can trust me, too. Maybe we can—you know—work something out." She looked at him hopefully. If he liked her—and that kiss sure felt like it—this was his chance to confess, and change his erring ways. She was ready to forgive. He was a private investigator, probably struggling to make a living. He couldn't be too choosy about his jobs in this tough economic climate.

John frowned in perplexity. What was she suggesting, that he join forces with Hal? "Work something out?" he said.

"Yeah. Think about it. We'll talk tonight. Bye." She stood on tiptoe again to plant a light kiss on his cheek. "You missed a spot," she said, brushing the little patch of whiskers. "But don't shave it off. It's sexy."

Then she was gone, jauntily swinging her big black purse.

John went back into his room, his finger playing over the little patch of whisker. Sexy, she said. He glanced at himself in the mirror and was disgusted with the moonish smile on his face. He pulled himself back to attention and opened his suitcase. She'd had the gun out. It wasn't wrapped up the way he'd left it. He went into the bathroom and opened his toilet case. "Damnation!" The Silly Putty was gone.

Chapter Five

"I think you went overboard, Hal," Sally said, when she met her uncle back at the apartment. "The phone call was enough. You didn't have to send in the cavalry as well. John probably smelled a rat when that bellboy showed up."

"Takes one to smell one," Hal said gruffly. He knew he had overreacted, but he felt responsible for Sal's safety, since she was working for him.

Sal felt herself bristling in John's defense and willed down an angry retort. "Anyway, he's coming tonight. Shall I get a start on answering that fan mail?"

"You'd better. It's piling up. Use the usual form letter. Wonderful things, computers. Each letter looks like a personal reply."

"I make each one personal! I change a few bits of the form to suit the fan. I'm always careful to answer any questions. What'll I tell Lottie Faraday this time?"

Lottie was an aggressive fan who had decided, sight unseen, that she was in love with Hugo VanAark. She invited him to visit her in San Francisco, hinted she'd love to visit him—anywhere, anytime—and occasionally proposed marriage to him. As she was also the president of his California fan club, she had to be handled with kid gloves.

"Just tell her I'm leaving the country for an undetermined length of time."

"Better make it a long trip or she'll suggest joining you."

"Tell her the Middle East. She'd have trouble getting a visa to go there. And tell her I'll remember her fondly when I'm broiling under the sun of Araby. That should hold her for a few weeks. Oh, and be sure to thank her for the tape of that caterwauling she sent."

Lottie changed careers frequently. At the moment she was singing with a rock band called The Fault Line.

"Ingrate! Some of the cuts were pretty good, especially one called 'Charade.' You should give a listen to it," Sally said.

"Are you forgetting she invited me to invest in producing the record? Ten thousand, she thought would be enough."

"It might not be such a bad investment. She's sending it to a couple of record companies. Lottie Faraday might be famous one day—more famous than you," Sally added, as she was in a bad mood.

"What is the world coming to when those rock people are rewarded more generously than true creative artists?" he scoffed.

"Gee, I don't know, Hal. It seems to me you and Shakespeare are doing okay for yourselves."

Hal studied her a moment. "I definitely smell a sour romance here. You're overdue for Italy," he said as he left.

Sally went to the office and began answering the fan mail. There were a lot of letters, and by the time she got to Lottie's, it was nearly time for dinner. Since Lottie was a special case, she saved her for the last and didn't use the form letter. She wrote:

Dear Lottie,

Thank you so much for the tape. It was a revelation. I particularly enjoyed the subtlety of "Charade." Unfortunately I won't be able to send you the ten thousand dollars, but I wish you every success in your new career. I'm leaving for the Middle East shortly and will be sure to take it with me for further study.

Mrs. Locum poked her head in at the door and said, "Dinner's ready, Sally."

"Oh, thanks. I'll just save this letter and finish it tomorrow." She shut down the computer, removed the disk and went to freshen up.

Hal watched his diet as carefully as an aspiring model. While he nibbled on a few ounces of chicken and salad, Sally enjoyed a fuller meal. She buttered a hot crusty roll and added a deviled egg to her plate. When the fresh strawberries arrived, she put a dollop of whipped cream on hers and had a few butter cookies with it.

"Your arteries must be as clogged as a California freeway," he groused, and took his coffee black, with artificial sweetener.

"If you're really worried about your arteries, you should lay off the booze," she replied, unfazed.

"A man with no vices is like a lady with no waistline—uninteresting."

"Then you're safe, Hal," she grinned. "I'll put the fan mail in your office for you to sign. I'll finish Lottie's letter tomorrow."

Hal had his own private office off his bedroom. The noise of the printer bothered him. He needed total silence and isolation to create. When they left the table, Sally took the letters to him, then decided she had time to finish Lottie's letter. By the time she had printed it, it was too late to start the envelopes, so she just left the letter on her desk and went to get ready for the party.

She brushed her short curls back from her face and patted on a little powder to subdue her freckles. Since Hal liked a touch of glamour in his hostess, she had a full wardrobe. She chose a black dress with big white polka dots. The front had a demure V neckline and a white collar, but the skirt was short and flirty, and the back was practically nonexistent. She added a pair of oversize pearl earrings and sandals and was ready to greet the guests.

He gave one look and said, "You look like Daisy Mae."

She wrinkled her nose. "You're just jealous because my legs are better than yours."

"That is debatable," he said.

Soon the guests began arriving. She knew the crew from the university and recognized some of the others, by name at least, from the conference program. The guests came from all around the globe, but they all spoke English. Although the apartment was large,

it was overflowing by nine-thirty. John still hadn't
come. Sally was beginning to wonder if he was going
to stand her up.

As the guests entered the building, John McCallum
sat in his car, surreptitiously snapping pictures to be
sent back to CIA for identification if they ended up at
the party. Not everyone entering the building was going to Hal's apartment, of course.

Half an hour after he was supposed to be there, he
knocked at the door and Sal let him in. There was an
air of self-consciousness between them, after their in-
timate parting kiss. John noticed that her eyes lighted
up when she saw him, and her lips curved in a smile.
His heart beat faster at that smile.

"What kept you? Everybody else is already here,"
she said in a breathless voice.

"I got lost in the arboretum," he replied, with an
embarrassed shrug. "Couldn't find the exit for the
trees."

The university had a botanical tree garden as part of
its campus, where it monitored the condition of local
trees, and also grew some specimens from around the
world to study adaptation possibilities. Since the arboretum covered a hundred and sixty-five hectares, it
was best to stick to the trails.

"I know what you mean. It's not a good idea to go
with dark coming on. They should issue a bag of bread
crumbs, like Hansel and Gretel, so you can find your
way out."

"Good idea, but you'd better make it pebbles. The
bread crumbs wouldn't last long with all those birds.
An owl attacked me. I guess it mistook me for a mouse
or rabbit." He held up his hand. "No comments,
please." He peered rather shyly into the room.

"Come on in and I'll introduce you around. You might pick up some inside dope for your article." She tried to make that last speech sound natural, to lure him into thinking she believed he was a writer, but he noticed a quick, assessing glint in her eyes.

He made a show of discussing the environment with some of the other guests. It wasn't hard. Each one was eager to hold forth on his own area of expertise. Sally kept an eye on him while she circulated among the guests. Physically, John didn't stand out. He was tall, but soft-spoken and unassuming. He didn't fill a room the way Hal did. His light business suit was practically invisible amid the brightly colored saris and oc-. casional burnoose and black evening suit.

But her body seemed attuned to his presence, as if some silken cord held them together. She always knew exactly where he was. She'd glance across the room and see him, with his towhead inclined to one of the guests, listening intently, with that gleam of intelligence in his eyes. He seemed to be aware of the invisible cord between them, too. Often, when she was looking at him, he'd glance up and smile at her. Every time she felt that surge of pleasure.

He had a nice smile—it tilted up on one side and a dancing gleam would flicker in his eyes. He'd watch her for a few seconds, then return his attention to whoever he was talking to. After a while, she noticed he was usually listening, seldom speaking. Well, that figured.

The prettiest woman in the room was Dr. Shelby. She was a Ph.D. in the environmental field, working with MIT. Her specialty was coniferous trees. Her skin was like a rose petal, and her black hair was positively iridescent with health. She wore a custom-tailored white suit, but the severe cut of it only enhanced her femininity.

Sally knew Hal would fall for her like a ton of bricks, but she was surprised and not too happy to see John talking to her for a good ten minutes.

When John caught Sally's eye, he returned to her. "Boy, these people really know their stuff!" he exclaimed. "Did you know trees can manufacture their own drugs? When bugs attack them, they can secrete some kind of resin to kill them. Mind you, it takes them a few decades to produce the drug."

"Smart old trees." She was relieved to hear it was trees they had been talking about.

They chatted for a moment, then John said, "I don't see Ranji here. Has he left already?"

"I believe he and Hal slipped off to Hal's office for a private discussion," she said. Ranji! John may be enjoying her company, but he wasn't letting it keep him from business. How did he even know Ranji was here? Had he been doing a stakeout? Ranji and Hal had been in the office ever since he arrived.

"They'll be out soon," she said. "I smell melting cheese and lobster. It's nearly time to eat. In fact, I'd better give Mrs. Locum a hand with the serving."

"Can I help?"

"Just work on your appetite," she said, and went to the kitchen.

For the next ten minutes she was busy helping Mrs. Locum put the finishing details on the meal. John began roaming around the apartment, trying to locate Hal's office. Using a trip to the washroom as an excuse, he wandered down a hallway. A door at the end was closed, with a light showing underneath. He walked up to it and listened.

He could hear voices, definitely Hal's, so the other must be Ranji's, but he couldn't distinguish the words. What mischief was the Silver Fox planning behind closed doors? Other people came down the passage in search of the washroom and he couldn't linger. He also wanted to get into the computer room. He returned to the living room, which gave a view of it. When no one was watching, he edged to the side of the room and across the hall toward the computer room.

The door was closed, but he was surprised to see it wasn't locked. He slipped in unobserved and flashed a light around. Enough computer power to run a large corporation. Computer hooked up to a modem. Fax machine, a wall of filing cabinets. Pretty substantial backup for a guy who taught one measly course in marketing!

He began riffling the files and found himself amid a welter of information on dairy cows. Yield, diet, weight gain, ancestry. He tried another, and discovered a list of European dairy farms. The next was more interesting. It was the accounting file, and the sums of money invested were staggering. This told John that the Silver Fox was raking it in, but it didn't tell him the source. He snapped pictures of a few pages with the miniature pocket camera concealed in his jacket.

He noticed a sheet of paper in the printer had some printing on it. He flashed his light on it. "Dear Lottie: ..."

The address was in the upper left corner. He snapped a picture of the letter, while a million questions buzzed in his head. Tape? What tape? It must be hot if the contact was asking ten thousand bucks! This Lottie was obviously a contact. And the Silver Fox was returning to the Middle East! Staynor would be interested to hear that! He took a look around the office for the tape. He didn't really expect to find it, and of course he didn't.

John knew he couldn't stay away from the party much longer without being missed. He put his camera back in his pocket, opened the door a crack to check, and slipped out unseen. The crowd was just moving toward the dining room. John attached himself to the tail end and went with them.

Sally stood behind a table, serving the guests from a sizzling hot plate. John noticed that Hal and Ranji had joined the throng. Since getting into Hal's office was so difficult, he decided he'd tackle Ranji's hotel room while he was at the conference tomorrow.

When he reached the serving table, Sally said, "I was beginning to wonder if you'd left without saying goodbye. You're the last one."

"I waited until the last so I could eat with you," he said. Her spontaneous smile told him she fell for it, and he felt like a jerk. "That looks good. What is it?"

"Kind of a mini lobster Newburg in patty shells. Scrumptious. And this is breaded eggplant," she said, putting some on two plates. "And my own personal favorite, hot cheese sticks. I'd skip the smoked oysters if I were you. They're out of a can, but the escargots are good. Oh, and we'd better have some of these fresh veggies for fiber."

"I guess this is another of your duties, playing hostess for your uncle," John mentioned casually.

"One of the more pleasant ones. I was working on the word processor all afternoon, answering letters. Hal's a computer illiterate. I'm trying to get him to take a course on word processing at the university.

Sometimes he pecks a few letters out himself, but I'm the main typist.''

John listened and did some thinking. If Sally did the letter writing, then she wasn't as innocent as he had hoped. She had probably written that letter to Lottie. On the other hand, the few letters Hal wrote himself might be the incriminating ones.

He still didn't know for sure that Sally was guilty. He'd send Lottie Faraday's address off to Washington tonight and let them find out who she was. A West Coast informant, obviously, finding out secrets and sending them to her boss on tape. And whatever she had sent, it was sending the Silver Fox dashing out of the country.

When they returned to the living room with their plates, Sally noticed that Hal had cornered the luscious Dr. Shelby. They both had a plate of crudités. They sat nibbling celery and raw carrots and cauliflower, while their eyes spoke of more interesting things.

Shortly after the coffee was served, the guests began leaving. There was a lecture at eight-thirty the next morning, and no one wanted to stay up late.

By eleven, everyone was gone except Dr. Shelby and John. Hal turned to his niece with a meaningful light in his eyes and said, ''Why don't you take John for a drive along the river, Sally? It's a lovely night. Martha wants to see those lithographs I picked up in Venice last year.''

Wants to see his etchings is what Hal meant. In other words, he'd appreciate a little privacy with Martha.

''Sure, Hal,'' Sally said. ''Are you interested, John?''

"I really should be going," John said. He had to get his film developed and send Lottie's name to the CIA. He had managed to snap a picture of Ranji as he came in, too.

"The night is young," Hal said.

John did want to be alone with Sally and was easy to persuade. As soon as they were out the door, Sally said, "We don't have to go to the river. There's not much to see at night. Hal just wants to be alone with his new catch, which is why I left, even though you wanted to go home. Listen, you go on. You're probably tired. I'll just drive somewhere and get some coffee."

"A bit awkward for you, being put out of the house at this hour of the night," John frowned.

"It's only eleven o'clock. And this isn't exactly a big, wicked city. I didn't have to leave. I could have just gone to my room. Hal never—you know. They'll just talk and have a drink."

"We'll drive around a bit," John said.

"I'll drive. I know the town, and it's a nice night for a convertible." John was quiet as they went to the parking garage.

They drove through the downtown, which was almost deserted at eleven o'clock. The restaurants and theaters and bars were still lighted, with a few people going in and coming out. "Just like Broadway, isn't it?" she laughed.

"I prefer this. I don't know how people can live in New York."

Sally stared at him. "You live there yourself. How do you do it?"

"On a permanent basis, I mean." He was thankful for the darkness that concealed his flush of annoyance at that slip. "Let's park somewhere quiet so we can talk."

"All right." She drove to the side of the road and turned off the motor.

But when they were parked, he knew he couldn't quiz Sally. Whatever her uncle was doing, she was probably in on it. She was a part of it, sharing those large sums he'd seen in the files. She liked being hostess to his parties, all decked out in her fancy clothes. She liked her fine foods, her horse, her convertible and her trips to Europe.

"It was a nice party," he said, since Sally didn't say anything.

"Good food, but the crowd wasn't my type."

John gazed at her intently. "What's your type, Sally?"

"Just plain folk—like you." Then she stopped. John wasn't the simple guy he was pretending to be, of course. She turned to him and said, "But you're not really plain folk, are you, John? You're after something, and I think I know what it is."

His first instinct was to deny it, but there didn't seem any point. "How'd you find out? You searched my hotel room?"

"Yeah. I saw the gun, and my Silly Putty, among other things. Why'd you take it?"

"I wasn't sure it *was* Silly Putty."

"What'd you think it was, a bomb?" she sneered.

John batted the question away impatiently. "Why do you do it? Just for the money?"

She had often asked herself why she didn't get on with a real career. She was an honors graduate in languages, and her present job didn't use half her skills.

"Hal needs me," she said defensively. "He's practically alone in the world."

"He can afford to buy any company he wants."

"You can't buy family. Besides, I kind of enjoy the work. It's exciting."

"That's one word for it. The Silver Fox," John said, shaking his head. "Whoever thought he'd be raising cows."

"You know he's the Silver Fox?" she exclaimed. "How did you find out?"

"We have our sources. I have to stop him, Sally. It's my job. We know he's working on a Middle East project."

Sally just sat, bewildered. "So what? It's none of Wigo's business what he does."

He didn't recognize the name Wigo, but he certainly didn't mean to tell her that. "So you know about Wigo," he said.

"Of course, we've known all along. You can just go back to New York and tell Wigo you failed. The project is ready to roll. The deal is down. You can't stop us, and you can't beat us to the draw."

John sat, trying to keep his jaw from dropping. What had he stumbled into here? "Wigo will be pretty upset," he said carefully.

"Serves them right. You should be ashamed of yourself, working for that second-rate publishing house. Plagiarizing is a crime, you know. We could set the cops on you."

John listened carefully, trying to hide his confusion. When he was unsure of his ground, he was careful what he said. "I don't know that I'd call it plagiarizing," he said.

"I don't know what else you'd call it," she retorted hotly. "You steal his book, and have someone hammer out a rip-off story based on Hal's ideas and knowledge."

Wigo, the publisher of men's adventure fiction. That's what she was talking about. John could hardly believe his luck. Miraculously, she didn't know he was with the CIA! She thought he was working for Wigo publishing. He might still pull through with his cover intact if he played it smart. "All right, you've found me out," he said humbly.

"That's a lousy trick, John," she said, but she seemed more hurt than angry. "I suppose you planned to steal his new manuscript?"

"No, just get a look at it," he said, scanning his mind to think how he could learn more without revealing he knew diddly himself. "What's he calling it, by the way?"

"I guess the title isn't a big secret. He's calling it *After the Storm*— you know, a follow-up to *Before the Storm*. What did you mean—you knew about his involvement in the Middle East?"

"We knew the new book was also set in the Middle East," he improvised hastily.

When there was a little pause in the questions, John sat, trying to assimilate what he'd just heard. The Silver Fox was Hugo VanAark. It hardly seemed fair for him to have garnered even more glory. VanAark's books always went to the top of the charts. Yet when John had digested it, it seemed logical. Who would know better than Harmon how things were done in the Middle East? He was obviously creative and imaginative.

In fact, the CIA was interested in VanAark, too. They knew he knew too much, but the connection had never been made with Harmon. That Harmon was Hugo VanAark, however, didn't mean he wasn't also spying for the enemy. That letter to Lottie, the tape, the ten thousand bucks, and the pending trip to the Middle East still looked highly suspicious.

"Well, you've blown my cover now," John said, and gave an apologetic shrug. "I'm really sorry, Sally. I don't enjoy doing this sort of thing."

"I know," she said, and took his arm. "I'm sure you must need the money, John. Things are probably tough in the private-eye business during this economic slump. But you'll drop this case, won't you? I mean you might as well. You can be sure the manuscript and disks are locked up tight as a drum in Hal's bedroom. I shouldn't be telling you this. You won't try to steal them?"

"Scout's honor," he said, putting his hand on his heart. "What chance would I have with that security system? I should never have agreed to take the case, but my rent was overdue, and I had car payments to meet."

"I knew it was something like that," she said, concerned.

"I really like the way you leapt to your uncle's defence. I thought for a minute there you were going to push me out on the sidewalk. When you like someone, you don't hold anything back." He noticed she was also quick to forgive. He liked that, too.

"I blame it on my red hair," she said, basking in the glow of his compliment, and the warm way he was gazing at her.

"And that's what you do for your uncle, Sal? Type his novels?"

"I do all kinds of other things. I help him with research and suggest ways to rev up his plots. I practically write some of the romantic scenes."

John felt a languishing sense of peace invade him. Sally was innocent. She was just her uncle's secretary for his writing. He should have known the Silver Fox was too much of a gentleman to involve a lady, and his own niece at that, in something dangerous and unsavory.

"What were you doing with the Silly Putty?" he asked.

"I was being Countess Sophia, planting plastic explosive in the minister's car. That's another thing I do for Hal. More to the point, why did you take it?"

He found himself momentarily speechless. "I was just curious. I couldn't imagine what you were doing with it and wanted to see if it really was Silly Putty. I loved Countess Sophia in *Before the Storm*," he added hastily to divert her attention from the Silly Putty.

"She was an old flame of Hal's. The one woman he loved, I think. I pretend I'm Sophia when I try out the tricky bits of his plots for him, to see if they can actually be done. He's very careful about that. You've read him, then—if you know Sophia?"

"I practically know him by heart," he said, with an easy conscience. Every agent read VanAark and dreamed he was that wiley.

All the little mysteries that had been bothering John were cleared up. The mysterious 'Countess,' the hoodwinking of the environment minister regarding his speech, the sneaking into his room.

"So your uncle is on to me?" John said.

"Are you kidding?" she laughed. "He's known since the night you followed me out of Graham Hall and cleaned your glass of prints at the apartment—to say nothing of my black purse. You dashed out of the apartment to meet Ranji as soon as you left me last night. Hal called Ranji to check."

So that was why she broke into his room, to see if he had got any information for Wigo from Ranji. "Who is Ranji anyway?" he asked.

"Just a spy friend from the old days. He's working for the environment now, but he's been in the Middle East more recently than Hal, and he gives him up-to-date information to use."

John felt that Sally believed it, although he doubted it himself. He felt guilty, exploiting her innocence, but he was sure Sally would understand. It would be painful for her to learn the uncle she loved so much was a traitor, but she would understand that he had to do his job. Even the Silver Fox would realize it. It was important to John that the Silver Fox understand that. You don't give up an idol that easily. John even wondered if it would be possible to persuade the Fox to go straight. Once he knew the CIA was on to him, he'd know his work was going to be difficult if not impossible.

"I'm really sorry, Sally," he said. "Now what do you say we go and look at that river your uncle mentioned?"

"More like a creek," she laughed. "He just wanted to be alone with Dr. Shelby. He's a pushover for those sophisticated women. Of course he was always too clever to let them get away with anything when he was in the field," she added loyally. She started the engine and headed for the river.

Her speech confirmed that she didn't know Harmon was still in the spy business. "I can see it's going to be tough living up to your uncle," he said.

Sally was happy to hear that little edge of jealousy. "You probably have interesting cases, too. It must be fun, being a private eye."

"Sometimes," he said. "But a lot of it is dull stakeouts. Now let's go watch the submarine races."

They drove down to the river and parked along its edge. The moon cast a giant flickering web of light on the black surface. Tall trees whispered to the night.

"What did you do in my hotel room, besides take back your Silly Putty?" John asked. He placed his arm along the back of her seat with his fingers playing in her hair.

"I looked for proof you were working for Wigo. Didn't find much."

"The Countess would be a useful helper for a private eye," he said, smiling down at her.

"Helper! I'm tired of being a helper. If I go into that business, I'll get my own license. In fact, I'm thinking of writing a spy book myself. I've learned a few tricks from Hal."

"We've all learned a few tricks from the Fox," John said, with a wistful note in his voice.

"Yeah, he's one of a kind, isn't he?"

"I'm glad you're his niece!" John said jealously. His arm tightened around her, pulling her head to his shoulder. "That's pretty stiff competition for a guy."

"It wouldn't be a problem. I'm not his type. The countess, maybe...." She peered up and saw John's face hovering above her.

"Countess, secretary—I'm not fussy," he said, and kissed her in the moonlight while an owl hooted menacingly from a tree. He was glad she didn't kiss like a jaded countess but like a young woman in love. She had obviously been raised with old-fashioned scruples. She'd only let him go so far.

After half an hour, Sally drove back to the apartment. John saw her to the elevator and kissed her good-night before going to his own car. As she went up in the elevator, she pondered how to tell Hal, and still make it possible for John to be allowed into the apartment. Hal was waiting for her at the door.

"Has Dr. Shelby left?" she asked.

"Yes, Martha is chairing a panel discussion tomorrow morning. She didn't want to stay too late. I'm ready for bed myself. Did you and John have a nice drive?"

"We have to talk, Hal," she said. She was glad he was in a good mood. The visit with Dr. Shelby must have gone well. "You were right," she said. "John is with Wigo, but we talked, and he's not going to continue with the case. He promised! And he's sorry, too."

Hal wasn't very disturbed. "I knew it! Well, if he's promised to be a good boy, you can invite him to Hilltop for the weekend. Martha is joining us, so you'll want company. Not much harm he can get into there. I do all my writing here, in my office."

She threw her arms around him. "Thanks, Hal. I'll ask him. I'll let you get to bed now. You'll want to look your best for Martha. Good night." She bounced up from the sofa, then stopped at the doorway and turned around. "It was a nice party," she said.

Hal wore the smile of a cat who's just had his fill of cream. "Yes, it was."

The only worry in Sally's mind as she prepared for bed was that John might not want to go to Hilltop now that he wasn't spying on Hal any longer. Maybe he'd have to get right back to New York and find a new case. When she heard Hal's howl, she thought he'd hurt himself and went flying to his bedroom.

He stood staring at the open diskette holder on his desk. "It's gone!" he said. "The *After the Storm* disk is gone. That bastard McCallum lifted it right out from under our noses. How the hell did he get into my private office? The door was locked."

Mrs. Locum, who was tidying up in the kitchen, came darting into the room. "Are you all right, Mr. Harmon?"

"Far from it. Something's been stolen from my office. You have a view of this hallway from the kitchen, Mrs. Locum. Did you see anyone lurking about here?"

Mrs. Locum looked uncertainly at Sally. "I did see Mr. McCallum standing by the door," she said. "But he wasn't trying to open it. He was just listening. He didn't see me as I passed by taking a fresh bucket of ice into the living room."

"He's got it!" Hal exclaimed grimly. "No wonder he agreed to drop the case. He's done his part, filched my novel. I'm calling my lawyer."

Sally stood, looking as if she'd been beaten with clubs. He had lied to her again! And she, like a dope, had believed him. She thought he was giving up the case for her, when he was only giving it up because he'd gotten what he wanted already. He had used her, but he wouldn't get away with it. By golly she'd show him!

"Why don't you call the hotel? Or call the police?" she said in a hard voice. "They might get him before he leaves."

"If he's worth his salt—and I grant you he's a better thief than I gave him credit for—the disk is already in the mail to Wigo, but I'll pay him a call," Hal said.

Sally said, "I'm going with you."

"No. You stay here, Countess. Phone him and talk pretty to him until I get there. Don't let on we know the disk is gone. If he still has it, that'll prevent him from hiding it."

Hal grabbed his keys and darted out the door.

Sally phoned the hotel, but there was no answer in John's room. He had probably left town already, dashing off to New York with Hal's novel on disk.

Chapter Six

It was about fifteen minutes later when Hal called the apartment on his car phone. "John's not at the hotel," Sally told him.

"I know. I've been there. He hasn't checked out. Where the hell can he be?"

"It might be best to wait for him there."

"I'll wait in his room," Hal said grimly.

"Why don't I join you?"

"No, wait for me there. I'll be home soon."

While Sally waited, her mind roamed over the evening. John had seemed so nice, she could hardly believe he had stolen the disk. Was it possible someone else had? Like the sultry Dr. Shelby, for instance? But she was a Ph.D. in environmental studies, what would she want with it? No, it was just her stupid old subconscious, trying to paint John innocent because she was attracted to him.

To help pass the time, she phoned the airport to see if John had booked a flight to New York. He was driving a rental car with Canadian plates, so he hadn't driven up from New York. She learned he hadn't booked a flight, or passage on a train. While she paced the living room, trying to think who else she could phone, Mrs. Locum came into the room.

"I'm sorry if I pointed the finger at your young man, Sally," she said. "But I did see him hanging around that corridor. Of course he isn't the only one who could have done it," she said with a sagacious look. Mrs. Locum was one of the few who knew of Hal's double life.

"Mr. Harmon was showing that doctor lady the etchings in his bedroom," she continued. "There's that adjoining door into his office. I heard her ask him if she could have a martini. He went into the living room to make it. That takes a few minutes. She was there alone."

"But why would she want the disk?" Sally asked.

"I just thought I should mention it," Mrs. Locum said, and left.

Wishful thinking, Sally decided, and clamped her jaw tight, because she had a nearly overwhelming urge to cry. It was half an hour later when Hal returned, and he was in a black temper.

"Did you see him?" Sally asked.

"Oh yes, I saw him, but he didn't see me. I also had a look about his room. The disk wasn't there."

"Why didn't you speak to him? You should have threatened to call the police."

"He wasn't alone," Hal said angrily.

"Who was he with?"

"Dr. Shelby," Hal said, and gave a cynical laugh. "I knew she was staying at the College Inn, too. I decided to pop in and surprise her. Fortunately I listened a moment at the door before knocking. I heard voices. I waited around a corner, and ten minutes later, McCallum came sneaking out."

Something tightened in Sally's chest. "They're working together?" she asked, as if she didn't give a damn.

"It certainly looks like it."

"Maybe it was just a friendly visit," Sally said. "I noticed them talking together at your party."

"No, it wasn't that kind of talk," Hal said. "I couldn't make out every word, but I did hear enough to realize it was all business. Wigo was mentioned and Hugo VanAark."

For some perfectly illogical reason, Sally was happy to hear it. She hated the image of John and Dr. Shelby being lovers even more than she hated John being a spy for Wigo.

"And I, like a fool, have invited her to Hilltop for the weekend," Hal said.

"But she's a Ph.D.," Sally said in confusion.

"I'll double-check that tomorrow. I checked up on young McCallum, by the way. He was parachuted into the conference at the last minute, which looks highly suspicious."

"Mrs. Locum mentioned Dr. Shelby was alone in your bedroom for a few minutes."

"Yes, I remembered that, when I saw them together. She may have done the actual heist, but they're in it together. His job was to work on you, hers to work on me. And they both succeeded admirably, didn't they, Countess?"

"Yes, they did," she agreed grimly. "But they might still have the disk. Why don't we go after them?"

"It's too late for that. I have a different plan," he said with a wily, vulpine grin.

The case looked impossible to Sally. For all she knew they were on their way to New York even as they spoke. But the Silver Fox was smiling, and that gave her hope.

"We'll invite them both to Hilltop," Hal said. "Martha has already agreed to come."

"She won't show, Hal. She'll be on the next plane to New York."

"I think not, my dear. She has no idea I suspect her. With fifty odd people at the party, any one of them might have done it. The novel stops at the most interesting point. She'll try to find out how I mean to finish it. I'll convince her the disk she took is useless. A discard that I decided not to use. I'll make her think the real disk is hidden away and have a little fun watching her try to get her hands on it."

"But then she'll know you know the disk is gone—"

"She'll know *a* disk is missing. You just casually mention to McCallum that I'm annoyed with you. You must have accidentally thrown out the disk. You don't know why I'm angry, because I had discarded that novel anyway. It was flawed. I got hold of misinformation and wrote a perfectly ludicrous book. Those who know anything about the Eastern situation would split their sides laughing if it was printed. McCallum will tell Shelby, and they'll both accept an invitation to Hilltop. You'll see."

"Gee, I don't know, Hal," she said uncertainly.

"What have we got to lose? They've got the damned novel. They'll steal the plot and have someone pound out an inferior version of it. It's our only chance. Not up to the challenge, Countess?" he taunted.

It was her acting abilities she was concerned with. She wasn't sure she could make John think she still cared for him, now that she knew the truth. But she was so furious that she agreed to give it a try.

"All right, I'll do it. I'll phone John tomorrow and invite him to Hilltop. He said he'd be interested in going."

"I'll give my lawyer a buzz as well, in case the matter goes to court."

Sally went to bed and Hal phoned his lawyer, even though it was midnight. Of course it was perfectly useless to try to sleep. She kept seeing John's sincere-looking, worried face as he apologized for working for Wigo. Slimeball. She'd show him. She could lie and put on an act as well as he could.

It would just be a slightly different role from Countess Sophia. She'd really lay it on thick. She'd have him eating out of the palm of her hand. She'd make him fall in love with her, then he'd be sorry he'd lied.

After a really lousy night's sleep, she felt like a wet noodle in the morning, but when the phone rang, she put on a phony smile and a syrupy voice.

"John, how nice of you to call. I've been thinking about you. I hope you don't have to rush back to New York—now that you've dropped the Wigo case, I mean," she added. "That was really sweet of you. I do appreciate it."

"I never should have taken it," he said quickly. "But since it's a Friday, I thought I'd stick around for the weekend—if I can see you, that is."

"Oh good! Then you'll come to Hilltop with us? We can go riding, and you can meet Shep."

"Did you tell Mr. Harmon about who I am?" he asked warily.

"Yes, but now that you've dropped the case, he doesn't hold a grudge. You have to make a living after all. He's done a few things he shouldn't have in his own life."

"That's very generous of him," John said. Suspiciously generous! Was the old devil really that obliging?

"He's a bit miffed with me," Sally said. "I goofed. He had part of a novel written, and I went and lost the disk. Tossed it out, I guess. There's such a pile of disks around the office."

"Oh?" John said, in a voice that was noticeably curious. "That sounds serious. I expect he has hard copy though?"

"I guess he kept it. Not that it matters. He's working on a completely different plot now. He gave up on that book. He got some faulty information from his sources. He said the book would make a laughingstock of him. He was sure glad he found out in time. It's just the idea of my having lost his disk that bothers him. I was going to erase it anyway."

"Maybe it'll turn up," John said.

"Yes, that's always possible. So, will you come to Hilltop with us? Please do. I'm really looking forward to it."

"I'd love to." After a moment he said, "Will anyone else be going?"

"Hal's invited a friend—that woman he was talking to last night, Dr. something or other. You know, the attractive woman in the white suit. That'll keep him out of our hair," she added insinuatingly.

"This gets better and better," John said. He was surprised and delighted that Sally was so friendly. He was afraid they'd have to meet in secret once she told Hal that story about him being from Wigo. "I'll apologize to him very nicely. I'm really looking forward to talking to the Silver Fox and Hugo VanAark, two of my all-time favorites heroes."

"Save a few minutes for me," she said.

"You're top priority. What time are we going?"

"I'll pick you up at the hotel around five, if that's all right?"

"That suits me fine. I'll see you then."

"Bye."

They hung up, and Sally gave a snarling look at the phone. Phoney! He didn't even ask what she was doing all day. They could have spent the afternoon together. He was probably going to spend it with Martha Shelby.

She went to find her uncle and said, "All set. I told John what you said I should, about losing the disk, and the novel being discarded. He's coming to Hilltop with us. Is Martha Shelby still coming?"

"Make that Martin Shelby," he said, with a sneer. "She's still coming. I was up early and dropped by the convention center to have a word with the secretary. The original list shows a Dr. Martin Shelby. They thought it was a typing error when a lady showed up. Of course I phoned MIT and asked to speak to Dr. Martin Shelby. His secretary told me he was out, but she didn't blink an eye about the Martin. I'm surprised that Wigo is so well organized. They found out who wasn't coming and parachuted that woman in his place."

"She must be a quick study! She's giving a lecture this morning, isn't she?"

"Yes. She must have got hold of Dr. Shelby's speech. Anyone can read, but the question period should be interesting. I think I'll go and watch her squirm."

"Sadist! I'd like to go with you, but I'm going to shadow John instead. Mind changing cars, Hal? He'd recognize my convertible, but he doesn't know your Porsche."

They exchanged keys. "Take good care of it" is all he said.

Sally drove over to the hotel and parked at the far edge of the lot. She spotted John's rented car and hunkered down to wait for him to show up. After half an hour, he came out and got into his car. She let a few cars get between them, then she followed. He drove out of town, heading east, toward Toronto. Now what was he up to? He wasn't taking the 401, which was the fastest and easiest way to get there. She thought a stranger would want to avoid the back roads, but he continued along Highway 7, passing through a few small towns en route. Rockwood, Acton—he was going to Georgetown! And that meant he was casing Hilltop.

Sally knew when the farm was coming up, and parked off the road. She got out and peered into the distance. Sure enough, he stopped at Hilltop. And he was taking pictures of it. Did he work for some yellow-journalism rag on the side? She could just see it, Hal's secret identity flashed across the scandal magazines, revealing his secret to the world. John focused his camera on the pool, a turquoise rectangle glimmering in the sun. He took pictures of the valuable herd of prize cows and the house.

She waited, and when he went back to his car, she turned around and drove back to Guelph. She soon spotted him in her rearview mirror, so she knew he was going back to town.

Hal returned from the conference at twelve sharp. "Well, did you have fun watching Martha squirm?" Sally asked.

He scowled. "She's good. Damned good. No one could stump her. My opinion of Wigo is rising by the minute."

"John drove to Hilltop and took pictures," she said, and mentioned her fear that he was working for a scandal magazine.

"He won't be in a rush to send that film off. He'll want more at home shots before he submits them. I'll pinch it while he's at Hilltop."

In the afternoon, Hal worked on the last few chapters of his novel, and Sally did what she always did when she was depressed. She went shopping at Stone Road Mall. Her great weakness was earrings, but she also bought a really skimpy bikini to make John fall in love with her.

At a quarter to five she drove to the hotel to pick up John. Hal followed in his car to get Martha Shelby. He hadn't found out yet who she really was, so continued using her given name.

John was wearing sneakers, a blue sports shirt the same cerulean blue as his eyes, and formfitting jeans that hugged his lean body like the skin on a peach. This was how Sally had been picturing him, with the sun turning his crisp tow hair a shimmering bronze. He was the picture of the all-American boy. Healthy, handsome, wholesome. It really didn't seem fair that he should also be such a sneak.

"Looking good, John," she said, letting her eyes linger on his broad chest. It was amusing to watch him blush.

"You don't look bad yourself," he said, and tossed one small suitcase in the back of the car. Then he got in beside her. "Is the farm very far away?" he asked.

She was tempted to say it hadn't moved since that morning, but she swallowed the urge. "Half an hour's drive." She leaned over and placed a light kiss on his lips. "You forgot to say hello."

"Hello!" he said, and pulled her into his arms for a longer kiss. Her treacherous body responded to his touch. Even knowing what he was, her pulse raced tumultuously. She drew back, before she forgot why she was here.

"I brought my bathing trunks in case there's a river or quarry nearby," he said.

Boy, he was good, too! Explaining in advance how he happened to have his trunks along. "There's a pool," she said.

"Really! I'm looking forward to that."

She reached out and squeezed his fingers. "I bought a new bathing suit, just for you," she said, smiling shyly. His blue eyes sparkled with anticipation. "I hope you like bikinis."

"Is it a yellow polka-dot affair?" he asked.

"No, blue, to match your eyes, but it's teeny-weeny."

John's arms reached for her. She turned demurely away and started the engine. His was already running. "Not before I drive," she said. "It's too distracting. We'll wait till later."

She watched as the Adam's apple in John's throat bobbed when he swallowed. He might be trying to use her, but he wasn't entirely immune to a flirting, bodacious woman. She'd have her revenge yet! "I can hardly wait," he murmured.

"I'll take you on my favorite ride tomorrow," she said, as they moved through the traffic. The office workers were heading home, and the roads were clogged. "There's a creek through the property. Silver Creek, it's called. It's very unspoiled and private. We can wade and try to catch crayfish."

"I'm surprised you have them this far north," John said woodenly. He wondered what had caused the change in Sally. She hadn't been this forward before. He liked her as a shy woman, but he found his hormones liked this more flirtatious side of her, too. Maybe Sally wasn't the young innocent he had thought.

"Yes, we have them. They don't grow very big in the colder water though."

"This is pretty countryside," he said, looking around. "Is it all rural?"

"We pass through a few small towns," she said. The same ones you passed this morning, John. "You might like to visit the Old Hyde House in Acton tomorrow. It really used to be a hide house."

"What did they hide?" he asked in confusion.

"Hide as in animal hide. It was an old tanning factory. They sell all kinds of leather and furniture and things. And they have a lovely dining room—Jack Tanner's Table—with exposed rafters a mile high, and a huge fireplace and windows in the roof and hanging plants all over."

"Acton? Is that near your farm?" he asked innocently.

"About ten miles this side of it."

Sally kept up the act all the way to the farm. She made a point of stopping right where he'd stopped and pointing out the pool. "That's where we'll be cooling off after our ride tomorrow," she said. "If we happen to need cooling off, that is."

He willed down the image her words called up. "And that must be the farm," he said, pointing to a lovely old redbrick gabled house, set at the end of an avenue of poplars. "The old Fox does pretty well for himself. Since he uses his real name, I'm surprised no one knows who he is. You'd think the scandal magazines would have found him out before now. Blown his cover."

"They'd probably pay a handsome price for pictures of all this," she said. "It's hard to imagine anyone being that hard up for money, isn't it? Hal figures he's safe, up here in Canada. Only a few very good friends know who he is, and none of them would be low enough to rat on him. That'd be a despicable thing to do."

"You don't have to worry about me. I won't squeal."

"I know *you* wouldn't do anything like that, John," she said, with a trusting smile.

"Does Martha know your uncle's Hugo Van-Aark?" John asked.

"I believe he planned to tell her this afternoon," she replied. "And that means he's serious about her. He wouldn't have invited her to Hilltop otherwise. We

don't invite anyone except *very* special friends here,''
she said, with a long, meaningful look. She noticed
John's discomfort with that remark.

He looked ill at ease, but he tried to smile. ''That's
very flattering, Sally.''

''Oh no! Flattery is insincere. I really meant it,
John.''

Then she continued along the highway and turned
in at the row of poplars.

Since Hal and Martha were close behind them, they
waited for them at the car. Almost before they got out,
a black-and-tan dog came bounding forward to greet
them with friendly yelps and wagging tail.

''I guess you know who this is?'' she said to John.

He reached down and patted Shep's head. ''Glad to
meet you, Shep. I've heard a lot about you. Sorry, I
don't have any corn on me.''

Soon Hal and Martha arrived, and they all went
into the house together. It was refreshingly cool inside but not dark. Sunlight splashed into an old-
fashioned living room decorated in early Canadian
pine furnishings. The dhurrie rug wasn't Canadian,
but its rustic charm blended with the furnishings. The
modern conveniences were disguised behind custom-
made furnishings. The TV and stereo were in a pine
cabinet with white porcelain knobs.

''Charming,'' Martha said, looking all around. ''I'll
just freshen up, then we'll have that drink you promised me, Hal.'' She was wearing a fuchsia sundress and
had her hair bound up in a polka-dot kerchief. With
big sunglasses, she still managed to look gorgeous.

''I'll speak to Mrs. Hudson,'' he said. ''The housekeeper. And perhaps you'd show Martha to her room,
Sally.''

"Would you like to freshen up too, John?" Sally asked.

They went upstairs with her. Sally put Martha in the guest room adjacent to her own bedroom, with John at the other end of the hall, across from Hal. If either guest decided to roam during the night, they'd be overheard.

She went back downstairs to the kitchen. Hal had stepped out and Sally spoke to Mrs. Hudson. She was a middle-aged local woman, wife of the man who ran the dairy. Her culinary expertise didn't match Mrs. Locum's, but she was a good cook, too.

"Will a steak and salad be all right for dinner, Sally?" she asked.

"Perfect. In fact, since it's such a nice day, we'll do them on the barbecue. I think we'll take the drink tray out there, too. Dr. Shelby might want to see the garden, since she's interested in that sort of thing."

"A doctor! Oh my!"

"Not a medical doctor," Sally said. "I'll get the drink stuff, Mrs. Hudson. Don't let me interrupt you. Mmm! Strawberries! Does that mean one of your delicious shortcakes, I hope?"

"I'm just about to set these cakes in the oven."

Sally arranged a tray of drinks. Martha had been drinking martinis the other night. She put gin and vermouth and olives on the tray. Hal would want beer. She put on three, since she felt like one herself, and John had mentioned liking beer.

When the others came down, Hal came in from outdoors where he'd been checking out the patio. He agreed it would be nice out there and they all went out.

"Allow me," John said, and carried the tray for Sally.

"This is quite a thrill," Martha said, turning to Sally. She had taken off the kerchief, revealing gold earrings the size of bracelets. Her jet black hair hung loosely down to her shoulders. "Hal has let me in on the secret of his alter ego. Or should I say pen name?"

"We just call it aka," Sally said.

"Guilty, as charged," Hal said, trying to look modest. "I began writing as a little divertissement when I retired, thinking to pass the time. Little did I ever dream it would become another whole career."

"And such a profitable one!" Martha said, her eyes glowing with admiration. "I just love Dirk Ransom. You really know the Middle East, Hal. Of course your days as the—" She came to an awkward pause.

"It's all right. John knows of my doings with the CIA," Hal said. "I told Martha," he added to Sally.

"As I was saying, your Silver Fox escapades give you an unequaled background for your novels," Martha said.

"Oh, as to that," Hal said, "I think the reading public are becoming a bit bored with the Middle East. I had another Eastern novel half done, but I discarded it. A rubbishy thing. The one I'm working on now is set in Japan. That's the up-and-coming country. Still the East, but the Far East, the Orient."

"What do you call it?" Martha asked.

Remembering what she had told John, Sally leaped into the conversation. *"After the Storm,"* she said.

"I may change the title," Hal added. "I feel *The Rising Sun* might do as well. It's still under discussion with my publisher."

"How fascinating!" Martha said, leaning forward eagerly. "Can we have just a tiny hint what it will be about?"

"It will deal with industrial espionage," Hal said. "But don't spread it around. I still have a deal of research to do. The government will be involved, and samurai warriors, and the Japanese mafia. Their criminals are legalized, you know. Extraordinary. They advertise in the newspapers when they're recruiting."

He chatted on, with his audience hanging on every word.

When he stopped for a breath, Martha said, "So the book you were working on, you feel it's flawed in some way?"

"It's just plain downright silly," Hal said emphatically. "I got very bad information from my Eastern sources. A pity, but there you are."

"And all that work—wasted!" Martha said.

"I wouldn't foist such a book on my reading public," Hal said. "Now who's for another drink before dinner?"

Mrs. Hudson brought out the steaks, and Sally volunteered to cook them, hoping John would help her. "We use mesquite," she said. "Hal doesn't like his steaks done over gas. I'm with Hal on that."

"And I'm with you," John said, reaching behind her to get the fork from the table. His hand brushed slowly over her back, lingering at her waist. "Can't think of a better place to be," he added, with one of his crooked smiles. Then his hand slid lower, and he gave her a playful little pinch before taking up the fork.

A flare of anger swelled, but Sally swallowed it and smiled provocatively. "Just look, don't touch—yet," she said.

"Can we get away after dinner?"

"Great minds think alike. There's a club in Norval, a little village a few miles from here. They have live music and dancing. I don't think Hal would like it."

"Good," John murmured, and began to place the steaks on the grate, while a slow smile crept across his face.

Sally was really getting to him. He had thought about it and concluded that once she was serious about a guy, she was a little freer in her manner. Free enough that he could hardly wait to be alone with her. They used the barbecue as an excuse to stay beyond earshot of Hal and Martha. Sally continued with her suggestive comments until John was sizzling as hot as the steaks.

Dinner was a great success. The steaks were pink and juicy, and the endive-and-tomato salad set them off perfectly. Mrs. Hudson had arranged a pretty table with a big bouquet of flowers from the garden.

"You'll love dessert, John," Sally said, when they were finished. "Prepare your sweet tooth for a real treat."

"Strawberry shortcake!" he exclaimed, as Mrs. Hudson brought it in. She had trimmed the cake so nicely that she wanted them to see it. Plump red berries, marinated in their own juice and sugar, nestled in the folds of mounds of whipped cream.

"I shouldn't! But I will," Martha laughed. "You're a tempter, Hal. How did you know I adore strawberries?"

"Doesn't everybody?" Sally sniped under her breath. She noticed that John and Martha acted as if they were virtual strangers. They hadn't said one word to indicate he had been in her room the night before.

When they had had dessert, Hal suggested they take their coffee into the living room. "I don't like sitting at a messy table," he said, and led them off.

As soon as they were seated, he said, "And what do you youngsters plan to do tonight?"

"I thought I'd take John to the Club 2000," Sally said.

Hal shuddered. "An infamous place," he assured Martha, who looked interested. She was about twenty years younger than Hal, but a little older than the people who went to the club. "Perhaps you'd like to watch a bit of television. They're rerunning the *Art of the Western World* series."

"Lovely," Martha said, smiling tenaciously. "And you must tell me more about your new book."

Hal just looked at Sally. "I'll tell you all about it, but you must promise not to tell a soul."

"I wouldn't dream of it!" she said.

John said, "Should I change to go to this club, Sally?"

"It's informal. You look just fine to me," she added, with a long, slow look from top to bottom. "But it's a little early to go yet. Would you like to take a stroll around outside? We can go to the stable and see the horses. You'll be riding Sunkist Miss tomorrow. Hal bought her, but he doesn't ride much. She doesn't get enough exercise."

They went out the back door, by the patio, to find Shep waiting for them. "Those lounge chairs look pretty tempting," Sally said. "I'm stuffed."

John took her hand and drew her on to one of a pair of chairs that were facing the west. "We'll just sit here and groan from overeating and watch the sun set," he said.

They kept holding hands, between the chairs, and when Shep realized he wasn't going to be taken for a walk, he settled comfortably at their feet.

"What a beautiful place," he said, sighing luxuriously.

The sun was sinking low behind a belt of cedars at the horizon. In the nearer distance, a herd of sleek holsteins grazed lazily. The old stone silo and the barn, painted a deep red, spoke of simpler days, when man was in harmony with the land. It seemed impossible that evil could thrive in such an idyllic spot. John thought that every tree and cow must chide Hal for his treachery.

"Does it remind you of your uncle's farm, in New England?" Sally asked idly.

"Nope. That's just a few scratchy acres. This is—" he threw out his other hand "—a garden of paradise."

"Yeah." And it even has a snake, she added to herself. To John she said, "Too bad the apples aren't out yet, huh, and I could tempt you."

"You're doing a pretty good job without apples."

"You ain't seen nothing yet," she said, and laughed lightly.

Chapter Seven

When Sally wanted to dance to live music, she went to Club 2000. It was the closest place big enough to attract bands people had heard of, and she liked the relaxed, casual atmosphere. The decor was simple: plain white walls, a bandstand, tables around the edge of the room, and a second level of seating above, with a view of the dance floor. The dim lighting concealed any architectural deficiencies.

When they entered, the room throbbed with the beat of a rock band. The moving lights, the band and the dancers were all that were needed to give a party atmosphere. Sally felt her spirits lift even before they found a table. The bottom floor was so crowded they had to go upstairs. This was less handy to the dance floor, but it provided a good view of the scene below.

They ordered a couple of beers and tried to talk above the din, but conversation was impossible. John held out his hand. She read his lips—"Dance?"—and nodded.

They went downstairs and squeezed their way onto the crowded floor. It felt good to just let go. All the pent-up frustration and anger that had been building up in her found a safe release in dancing. Talking was out of the question. Her whole body throbbed with the primitive beat of the music. The gyrating bodies flashed red and blue-green from the lights, adding a touch of surrealism to the scene.

While the music played, she just forgot her troubles and indulged in a bout of physical frenzy. She was surprised that John was such a good dancer. Tall, slender men were often awkward on the floor, but he moved with an easy grace. When the music stopped, John pulled her against him. He stood behind her, with his two arms encircling her waist. They were both breathing hard from the exercise. It felt good to have someone to lean on.

"These guys are good," he said, inclining his head to hers. She felt his breath in her ear, and a tingle shot through her. "Who are they?"

"Just a Rush cover band. They call themselves Fire Angel. Don't even ask what it means."

He placed a kiss on her ear, and something inside her exploded. "I know what it means," he murmured.

She turned to look at him. "What does it mean?"

"It means a redhead, with the face of an angel and a streak of the devil in her." He was smiling softly, not only with his lips, but with his eyes. That smile told her he meant her.

She batted her lashes shamelessly and said, "Which do you prefer, John, angel or devil?"

"Both are equally tempting. As long as the devilish side limits her machinations to me...."

She was glad the music started up again at that point, because she couldn't think of any clever reply. They finished the set and went back to their table. For two hours they danced, listened to the music, drank a couple of beers, and talked and flirted outrageously during the intermissions. Sally enjoyed every minute of it. It gave her a sense of power to be able to manipulate him, but by eleven o'clock she was tired of the charade.

She couldn't decide whether her plan had backfired or was working too well. John was certainly responding to her not-very-subtle overtures. He had moved his chair right next to hers so he could hold her hand. As the evening progressed, one arm found its way around her shoulders. From time to time he stole a kiss. The emotional temperature was skyrocketing, but where did they go from there?

He was going to expect more than a good-night kiss when he took her home. But even that wasn't the worst of it. She was convincing more than John with this little game. She was convincing herself, too. She liked it when he squeezed her hand, while gazing deeply into her eyes. Those long gazes seemed to carry a promise, and a challenge. And when his lips brushed her forehead or cheek, she felt as if live coals were fanning to flame inside her.

She hadn't found out a single thing that might help the case. The Silver Fox hadn't been mentioned since they left Hilltop. Why had she brought John here anyway? She could have flirted with him just as easily, and more safely, at home. The point of it all wasn't just to get revenge on him. It was to prove he and Martha were Wigo spies and to outwit them.

"Shall we try another dance?" John asked, when his drink was gone.

"Would you mind if we leave now, John? I'm getting a headache. All the noise and smoke..."

"We'll drive home with the top down. The fresh air will make you feel better."

They left at once and went out into the cooler night air. "Would you like me to drive?" John asked. "You can relax, try to get rid of that headache."

Her head really was beginning to ache, and it was thoughtful of John to drive. She was glad to let him. It allowed her to relax and think. When she laid her head back against the headrest, John pulled her closer to him. "Lean on my shoulder. It's softer," he said.

It wasn't, really, but she knew that was just an excuse to keep her close to him, and actually it did feel better. She found it awfully hard to go on mistrusting a man when her head was snuggled against his shoulder.

"That was fun," John said. "It feels good to cut loose at the end of the week."

He drove smoothly, not rushing the lights or screeching to a stop or insisting on passing everything on the road. When she complimented him, he said, "My dad taught me to drive. He said a gentleman—he still used that word—should drive as if a lady were holding a glass of water. A good driver would make sure she didn't spill a drop. I'm trying not to jar your aching head. How are you feeling?"

"Better," she said. She felt comfortable and safe with her head on his shoulder and the wind cooling her fevered brow. Overhead, a fingernail of moon and a myriad of stars looked down on them. She wished they could drive all night. While they were in the car, she didn't have to do much acting.

Hilltop was only a few miles away, and they were home all too soon. She figured John would make his move before they went into the house. The lights in the living room suggested that Hal and Martha were still up, so this was their last chance for privacy. He parked in the driveway, off to the side of the house where a stand of lilacs and a big maple tree provided shadow. The lilacs had faded, but the cloying sweetness of hyacinths perfumed the air.

John turned off the engine and handed her the keys. He didn't lunge at her, or seem to be in a predatory mood. He just asked in a nice, concerned way, "How's the headache now?"

"A bit better," she said, poised for it to become worse if he turned overly amorous.

"I recommend two aspirins and call me in the morning. I want you hale and hearty for our ride."

"A good idea," she said, and breathed a quiet sigh of relief.

When John got out and opened her door she realized that, while she was relieved, she was also just a tiny bit disappointed. Wasn't he even going to kiss her good-night?

"Should we put the top up, in case of rain?" he said.

"It's not going to rain. Look at that sky." The sliver of moon silvered the trees and meadows. "But it might be a good idea to keep the raccoons out," she added.

They put up the top and looked at each other, rather self-consciously. "Shall we go in?" Sally said.

"In a minute. This country air smells so fresh and clean after being at that club. It does your lungs good. Your head, too," he added, smiling sympathetically for her headache.

They just stood a moment, holding hands, gazing up at the stars and listening to the whisper of the leaves and grass. Then John drew her into his arms, in the shadows of the big maple tree, for one good-night kiss, that was long and sweet and tasted as innocent as the clear sky above. It felt like a promise, or a commitment.

Then they went inside. Hal sat alone in the living room, reading the newspaper. "Did you have a nice time?" he asked.

"A lovely time," Sally said. "Has Martha gone to bed?"

"She just went up. Would you like a bite to eat? Mrs. Hudson's gone to bed, but there's cold meat and cheese if you'd like to make John a sandwich, Sally."

"Sally has a headache," John said. "I'm fine. I'll turn in now myself. Good night, Hal. Sally."

He left, and Hal lowered his voice to a conspiratorial whisper. "I took a good root through McCallum's room. Of course he didn't leave anything incriminating behind. He doesn't have the disk. I opened his camera and exposed the film. Let him snap away to his heart's content. I couldn't get into Martha's room, but I invented such a good plot for the imaginary Japanese book that I've half convinced myself I'll write it next. I think she swallowed it."

"I didn't have any luck, either. You can't do much talking at a dance club."

"Was he asking a lot of questions?"

"Not really. What kind of questions do you mean?"

"I mean questions like where I do my writing. They must be dying to get a look at the Japanese book."

"Nothing like that. I already told him your office is in the apartment."

"Martha played the admiring fan to perfection. Where do I get my ideas, and how do I write? Do I use a pen or typewriter or word processor? How far have I gotten with the Japanese book? I told her I did all my writing in the apartment. I'm rather sorry I told her that. If I could lure her into indiscretion here and catch her red-handed . . ."

"She's too clever to leave herself open like that."

"Ah, but she doesn't know I'm on to her. That's our trump card, Countess. I know she's very eager to see what she can discover. I left her alone for fifteen minutes, claiming I had to go to the barn to see Hudson. She made a beeline for my office. She didn't find much there. Just my accounts for the farm and my passport—which doesn't show any trips to Japan. I made a point of telling her I hadn't been there yet."

"How'd you spy on her?"

"I ducked outdoors and peeked in the window. She was using a flashlight, doing a quick rustle through my desk. She was idly flipping through a magazine when I came back. I don't think we're going to learn much from this pair. We'll just hammer away at how the Middle East book is junk, and hope Wigo doesn't try to use it. Meanwhile my lawyer is preparing a suit against Wigo if they do try anything."

"Yeah, I guess that's all we can do—unless you want to set a trap," she said reluctantly. She realized she didn't really want to get John in a lot of trouble.

"Don't look so sad, Countess. Something will come up. Their being here adds a certain fillip to the weekend. It almost makes me regret giving it all up—the excitement of espionage. Martha is a worthy foe."

"And so pretty."

"Pretty? Nonsense, she's more than pretty. She's beautiful. I managed to rifle her purse when she went to make us a drink. She has full documentation for Dr. Shelby. Driving license, credit cards—the works. She must work for a very high-powered agency. A small operator doesn't have that sort of resources. And it was all done quickly, too. Martin Shelby only pulled out of the conference at the last minute. Wigo hires the best."

"They're good," she agreed.

"Very good—but not good enough to outwit the Silver Fox."

"You're the best, Hal," Sally said, and went up to bed.

Her room at the farm was rustic and cozy. The simple whitewashed walls held the memorabilia from her university days: a poster of Mel Gibson, looking sinfully gorgeous, with blue eyes like John's; a cork bulletin board covered with a pastiche of photos and notices of old dances; a corsage turned brown from age. She had bought the braided rug at a church bazaar, and the crocheted afghan on her bed came from her old room at home. She and Hal had found the brass bed at an auction sale, and the dresser and vanity were old without being antique.

The room always gave her a warm glow inside, but its charm failed her tonight. She couldn't stop thinking about John and Martha. If Martha was good—and she was—Sally felt John was just as good. He played his part superbly. She could almost believe he really cared for her. He was flirtatious when that was her mood, and when she pretended she had a headache, he fell in line by feigning concern. He wasn't doing anything to jeopardize his welcome. No danger of his being an amateur.

Hal said there wasn't much they could do except keep watching and listening and trying to catch John and Martha in a lie. And since this role of flirt she had adopted was becoming such a burden, Sally decided she'd abandon it. She couldn't go on having headaches all weekend. She and John would spend a fair bit of time alone together, and that could lead to trouble if she didn't cool it.

What puzzled her was Hal's easygoing attitude. She thought he would have wanted to stir things up a little, but he didn't go for her idea of setting a trap. Was it possible he was falling for Martha, too? They were a fine pair of spies! Hal always said getting emotionally involved was the mark of an amateur. It clouded the reason and warped judgment. But she didn't seem to have any control over her heart. She was already emotionally involved, and she'd just have to remember that John wasn't.

She was so drained that she slept well, despite her worries. In the morning, slivers of dazzling sunlight slipped in around the edge of her window blinds, painting an abstract design on the walls and ceiling. It was another sunny day. She'd been hoping for rain, so she wouldn't have to ride with John.

She showered and dressed in jeans, a cotton shirt and her riding boots. When she went downstairs, the others had already gathered for breakfast. The enticing aroma of bacon and coffee hung on the air. She gave the bacon a pass and had orange juice, scrambled eggs and toast. Martha was nibbling daintily on whole-wheat toast fingers, but the men were eating everything.

John rose to draw her chair. "Good morning, sleepyhead. How's the headache?" he asked. A shadow of uncertainty hovered about his smile until she announced it was gone.

"Good! Then we can have our ride. It's a beautiful day for it."

John looked right at home in his tan chinos and faded checkered shirt. She was afraid his sneakers wouldn't give him much grip on the stirrups. Hal offered to lend him his riding boots and helmet. Over breakfast, Hal amused them with stories of riding camels in the desert.

"Think of it as being astride a smelly, jiggling, foultempered horse with a lumpy back, eight feet off the ground," he said. "They're contrary devils. A mule is nothing to them. I've ridden plenty of mules in my day, in Eastern Europe."

"Such an interesting life you've had," Martha sighed, looking at him adoringly. "And next you'll be off to Japan. No danger of camels or mules there."

"Pedestrians and motor traffic are the villains in Japan, I understand. Tokyo is ridiculously overcrowded. I'm looking forward to it."

"I'd love to go myself," Martha said at once. "We don't know as much as we should about their ecological practises."

Hal didn't offer to take her along, but he looked as if he'd like to. Hal did most of the talking at breakfast. As soon as it was over, he invited Martha to tour Georgetown with him.

"We have to walk off those calories. I shouldn't have indulged in that bacon, but then a man must moderate even his moderation."

"Cleverly put!" Martha complimented.

He smiled his thanks. "Georgetown is a quaint little place. We'll avoid the mall and visit the old downtown. We have rather a nice library and art gallery, converted from an old Gothic church. There are a few antique shops, a bookstore. Oxbow Books carries some fine old volumes. I like to browse there. And of course we have some shops with ladies' clothing. I think we'll find someplace we can get an ice-cream cone later."

"It sounds charming," Martha cooed, as if there were nothing she liked better than browsing through small-town shops.

Sally got Hal's boots and the two helmets and met John in the kitchen. Hal's riding boots were handmade of Spanish leather.

"I feel like a conquistador in these!" John laughed.

"Do they fit?"

"My left foot pinches a bit, but it's worth it. And I won't be doing much walking. Beautiful boots!"

"You'd better put on the helmet, too," she said, adjusting her own.

They were both regulation close-fitting black riding helmets. John looked at it askance. "That's not my style," he said. "It's a woman's helmet. Looks great on you."

"Men wear them, too. They're unisex."

"I hate unisex. *Vive la différence.*"

"Vanity," she scoffed, but when he hung the helmet on the back of the chair she saw he wasn't going to wear it. "Let's go, then," she said. Fortunately Hal's horse was docile.

Shep was waiting for them at the back door. They had to pet him and play with him for a while before leaving.

"You must hate to have to leave him here when you go to the city," John said.

"I do, but our apartment doesn't allow dogs."

"I can't have one in my apartment, either. It's really not fair to the dog to leave it alone in a couple of rooms, or even tied up all day in a backyard with a rope around its neck. Talk about a dog's life! Dogs need a place like this to roam." He was rubbing Shep's ears just the way he liked. It was easy to see he really liked dogs. Shep liked him, too, and he was fussy about who he let rub his ears. That was something in John's favor anyway.

"Why don't we let him come with us?" he suggested.

"He usually comes with me when I ride alone."

"I'm glad to hear it," he frowned. "Is it safe for you to ride alone? What if you had an accident?"

"Like I said, Shep usually comes with me," she repeated, as they headed for the stables. She noticed that he was either genuinely worried about her, or playing his part exceedingly well.

Fandango was a trim filly with a chestnut coat and a white blaze on her forehead. She whickered in pleasure when she realized she was being taken out. Sunkist Miss was a little frisky, too. If Mr. Hudson didn't ride her, she didn't get ridden. Hal had a handsome riding outfit, which he occasionally put on to ride along the edge of the road to show off, but he didn't really like riding. He preferred fast cars.

John ran his eyes over Sunkist Miss and patted her to let her become familiar with him before mounting. "This lady isn't getting enough exercise," he said. "She's carrying more flesh than is good for her."

Sally noted that he really did know something about horses. She wondered if his uncle had that farm in New England, or if everything he had told her had been lies.

She used the riding block to mount; John just put his toe in the stirrup and flung himself into the saddle with a practised air.

"That way," Sally said, and led him off along the edge of the fenced pasture where the herd of holsteins were grazing. The sleek, pampered super-cows hardly bothered to look up from their grazing.

They began at a trot, and when she saw that John was a competent rider, she increased the pace to a canter, then to a gallop. Shep ran alongside, occasionally barking from pure joy. They rode together through the meadow spangled with dandelions and buttercups and dotted with trees. The sun was warm on their shoulders, and the breeze cooled their faces. John's hair danced in the wind.

Conversation was not only difficult but unnecessary. Each sensed the other's joy in the ride. The communion of man and beast and nature made for a perfect outing. The pleasure was increased by sharing it with someone who obviously appreciated it.

"Does your uncle own all this land, or are we trespassing?" John called, when they had ridden a few miles.

"This is the Hudson's land. They let us ride here, but we'll have to skirt the cornfield. It isn't enclosed."

She led the way around a field of sprouting corn laid out in neat rows. Farther along they passed an apple orchard. "This is glebe land," she said. "It belongs to a church. The creek is just over there."

"We'd better give Sunkist Miss a rest. She's panting," John said.

They slowed to a trot and entered a path through a stand of cedars leading to the creek. A gurgle of silvery water meandered idly through the countryside. Willows trailed their ribbons into the water. From the treetops the chirping of birds filled the air. The sky was a deep Wedgewood blue, spotted with marshmallow clouds.

They dismounted and went to toss pebbles in the stream. Shep insisted on trying to retrieve them, then came out and shook the water from his coat, splattering it in all directions.

"This would be a nice place for a picnic," John said, gazing all around. "Private," he added, casting a questioning look at Sally.

She knew what that look meant. "Shall we ride farther, or go back?" she said, pretending not to notice his mood.

"Isn't it *yet,* yet?" he asked, taking her two hands in his.

"What do you mean?"

"Yesterday when you were flirting with me, you said I ain't seen nothing yet. I took it as a promise of greater things to come."

"Oh, that," she said, pulling her hands away and laughing nervously. "I was just kidding around."

"Trifling with my tender emotions?" he said, grinning. He advanced a step closer. She backed away.

"That's a good way for a woman to get herself in trouble," he said with mock menace.

"A good thing I brought my guard dog, huh?"

Shep had picked up the scent of a rabbit and taken off, abandoning her. He went flying away with a happy yelp.

"Shep doesn't seem to think I'm a threat." He took another step forward. Sally stepped back.

"What's the matter?" he asked. "Had a change of mind? Or do I mean heart? Or do you feel another of those convenient headaches coming on, now that we're alone?"

"It's time to go back," she said.

"No hurry." He advanced. She retreated. Suddenly a truly diabolical grin seized his lips. She didn't trust that grin. She took another step back and felt herself sliding down the slippery bank into the creek. John lunged and saved her, just as her boot hit the water.

He pulled her out and set her down on firm ground, gripping her upper arms in his two hands. His head hovered inches above hers. His blue eyes glittered with amusement and something more sinister, that she thought might be anger.

"Let that be a lesson to you, Miss Glover, not to retreat when you should advance," he said. And pulling her into his arms, he lowered his head to hers.

It wasn't the gentle kiss of yesterday. His lips were hard and demanding. His arms wrapped around her, forcing the air from her lungs. She felt her breasts thrust against his hard chest. There was a fierceness in the embrace that frightened her, even while her blood rose in excitement. Then, as quickly as he had grabbed her, he pushed her away.

She just stood, gasping in surprise. John scowled and said something she found totally irrelevant. "You lead a very privileged life, Sally. Do you know that?"

"What do you mean?"

"That fancy apartment, the farm, horses, the convertible."

"I know that," she said defensively. "Don't think I don't appreciate it. My folks weren't exactly wallowing in money, you know. I never lived like this before Hal came along. Sometimes I feel quite guilty about it."

"Maybe you're doing something you shouldn't. People don't usually feel guilty for no reason."

She just looked, trying to figure out what he meant. Was that a dig about leading him on, then suddenly freezing up? He was a fine one to talk! He was doing a lot worse than that.

"Maybe I'm not the only one who should feel guilty," she retorted.

Shep came bouncing back and deposited a grungy old red ball at her feet. Glad for the diversion, she threw the ball and Shep ran off to retrieve it. She waited for John to defend himself, but he didn't say anything. He looked as if he was sorry he'd opened that particular can of worms.

Next John threw the ball. After a few tosses he said, "Shall we go?"

"Sure, I've had enough."

John was quiet on the way home. She could see he was in a bad mood, and she could hardly blame him. But he wasn't exactly innocent, either. They stopped for a while to look at Hal's cows. Some of them had calves with them. A few calves came to the fence to moo a welcome, but Shep barked in excitement and sent them scampering away.

"We'll have time for that swim before lunch," she said, to try to establish a more harmonious mood.

"We don't have to cool off much after all, do we?" he said, with a brow lifted ironically.

"I'd say it's chilly enough," she said, "but I'm going to swim anyway. You're welcome to join me."

They rode to the barn and unsaddled the horses, then brushed them down, without speaking. She noticed John groomed Sunkist Miss with real care and concern. The strong hands holding the brush stroked her flanks and neck. He wasn't just doing this because it had to be done; he enjoyed every minute of it. When the mare was smooth and glowing, he ran his bare hands along her conformation. Then he put the brush back.

"That was a good ride. Thanks," he said curtly.

"You can take my car if you'd like to drive into Georgetown. You might meet Hal and Martha there."

He looked surprised. "I thought we were going to swim?"

"You didn't seem very interested," she reminded him.

"No, Sal, *you* didn't seem very interested—in me." He gave an accusing look and went toward the house. Sally lingered behind a moment to ponder his sharp words. He stopped at the back door. "I'll put my bathing trunks on and meet you at the pool."

She kicked a stone out of the way and scowled at it. What was he trying to do? Making her feel guilty, with his darned innocent blue eyes. Looking as if she'd hurt him. . . .

Well, that was what she wanted all along, wasn't it? To make him care for her, then laugh in his face. Someplace along the way, things had gone wrong. John was just angry. She was the one who was hurting. And Hal didn't seem to be doing any better than she was.

Chapter Eight

In her bedroom, Sally looked assessingly at the skimpy blue bikini she'd bought to impress John. It was so small she could hold both pieces in one closed hand. It was the kind of suit that would leave an awful lot of Sally Glover showing. Too obvious, she decided. Besides, she'd given that game up as too dangerous.

The suit wasn't a complete waste. It'd be fine for the Italian Riviera, but Hal might not like it. She bit back a smile when she realized how many excuses she was making for not wearing it. Hal would hardly bat an eye if she went topless. The truth was she was shy to appear virtually naked in front of John.

She'd never have the nerve to wear the darned thing. She changed into a one-piece suit designed for swimming, not sunbathing or driving men wild, picked up a towel and went into the hall.

Since John was her guest, she decided she should knock at his door and go to the pool with him. The gesture might at least temporarily shore up the rent in their relationship. Not a solution but a quick fix to make the visit less uncomfortable. His door was wide open, the room was empty. He was quick!

She went down the hall and glanced in at the open bathroom door. Also empty. Of course he'd have closed it if he was changing there. Martha's door was open, too. Hal was the only one who'd bothered to close his. She ran downstairs and into the kitchen.

"I guess John's already gone out to the pool?" she said to Mrs. Hudson.

The housekeeper glanced up from the sink where she was cleaning vegetables. "Why no, Sally. He didn't come through this way."

"I see."

It was odd he'd gone out the front door, when the pool was at the back of the house. The hair on her neck suddenly rose in suspicion. Where was he, and what was he doing? She took a peek in Hal's office. Not there. She kicked off her sandals and went back upstairs, very quietly. John was just coming out of his room.

"All set?" he asked, as cool as a cucumber. "I had to stop and put a Band-Aid on my toe. Sorry if I kept you waiting, but Hal's riding boots raised a blister. Too small for me—and here I thought I could never fill his shoes."

"That's too bad about the blister," she said. He had been in Hal's room. There was no place else he could have been. All the other doors were open and the rooms empty. There was a Band-Aid on his toe. He was very thorough, but she doubted that it was covering a blister. It was just an excuse for taking so long to change.

"No hurry," she said, trying to sound natural. "The others aren't back yet."

John smiled his old innocent smile, while his eyes skimmed over her bathing suit, down to her legs. "I had my hopes up that you'd be wearing the bikini," he said.

"Will a drink do instead?"

"Where did you plan to wear it?"

She bit back a sharp retort.

To judge by that scowl, he figured she intended to throw it in his face. For some reason, Sally had stopped coming on to him, and he didn't know whether he was glad or sorry. But he knew that he had to behave politely, since he was a guest. "I'd love a drink, thanks."

"There should be some soda in the fridge." She turned to go downstairs.

John held her arm. "I think I preferred the tease, even if you had no intention of coming through on those unspoken promises," he said. It was her cue to explain. She just looked embarrassed. John continued. "If I offended you at the creek, I'm sorry, Sally. What do you say we go back to square one? Nice girl, nice boy. No tricks."

"I'm not a girl," she said.

"I'm easy. Nice woman," he smiled, although it was hard to continue his polite facade when she was so uncooperative.

"But are *you* a nice man?" she asked, and was sorry she'd revealed her anger.

"I told you, Sal, I'm not working on the Wigo case. If you've come across some sort of evidence or something—well, I'm not the only stranger in the house, am I?''

Sally felt he had hit a new low. Now he was ratting on his accomplice. What new scheme was this? Divert her suspicions to Martha, so that he was perfectly free to spy? She longed to tell him Hal knew he and Martha were working together, but she managed to control the impulse.

"Don't mind me," she said. "I'm just hot and tired after that ride. I'll feel better after a swim.''

"Well at least you don't have a headache," he said, and they went down to the kitchen.

They got two cans of cold soda pop and went out to the pool. Mrs. Hudson was a keen gardener. Big pots of flowers formed a backdrop to the glimmering water. She had planted rosy pink trailing geraniums and ivies, to match the pink sun umbrella and lounge cushions. Delicate lobelia tumbled in a froth of lace amid the greenery.

Half a dozen lounge chairs were placed around the umbrella table. They sat and sipped their drinks. A raucous blue jay was busy keeping the sparrows and smaller birds away from the bird feeder.

"That darned jay thinks he owns the bird feeder,'' Sally said, and chased him away.

"You're really in a snit today. Even the birds aren't safe. What's the matter, did you get up on the wrong side of the bed?''

"He always does that," she said. "And if it's not him, it's the squirrel. The sparrows are lucky if they get a crumb.''

"If he comes after my soda pop, he's had it,'' John said, laughing at her temper.

It was hard to keep her anger and vigilance up in such idyllic surroundings. Beyond the pool, a fence of cedars swayed lazily in the breeze. A pair of finches played hide-and-seek among the branches. Flashes of golden wings fluttered to reveal their whereabouts. No other farms or houses could be seen, just spreading greenery and the blue sky arching above. She and John might have been alone in the universe.

They had half their drink, then swam back and forth in the refreshing water. Sally floated on her back and watched as John tried a few dives from the diving board. It had a vicious kick. After one disastrous belly flop, he had to try again, to redeem his self-respect. The second one was a neat jackknife.

When they came out, John dried her back for her with slow, sensual strokes of the fluffy towel. It was more a massage than a simple drying. He kept it up long after she was dry. It felt so good she didn't want him to stop. But she didn't want to start imagining he liked her, either, that he was using the towel as an excuse for touching her. She moved away.

"What are you trying to do, remove my skin?" she said.

"Talk about ingratitude! I was giving you a massage."

"With a towel?"

He set the towel aside, but his fingers continued moving over her back in languid, caressing circles. The warmth of his fingers clung to her naked flesh, leaving a trail of heat in their wake, until she felt she was being branded.

"If you have some suntan lotion I'll use it instead," John said in a smoldering voice that had nothing to do with lotion. It was burred with desire.

His fingers grazed up her back to her shoulder and cupped it firmly.

"I don't need it. We're under the umbrella." Her voice sounded choked.

"It'll feel good," he tempted, squeezing her shoulder harder. "Very good," he added huskily.

That was exactly what she was afraid of. Now that she'd stopped flirting with John, he seemed determined to tease her. "You rub too hard," she said.

"I can be gentle." He directed a penetrating gaze that seemed to go straight through her and read her every thought. There was an implicit question in his eyes.

When she didn't answer, he dropped his hand and said, "I think what you mean is that I rub the wrong way." After that statement he reached for his drink.

She was saved from replying by the arrival of Hal and Martha, back from their little trip.

"It was lovely," Martha said. "Like a little town out of the last century. So pleasant to see some stores other than the usual chains in the malls. Oh, and we saw a wedding at that old stone church on the corner, a formal white wedding."

"June is the traditional month for weddings," Hal said, with a thoughtful look at Martha.

That look worried Sally very much. Was the Silver Fox going soft in his old age?

Mrs. Hudson brought Hal and Martha some Bloody Marys and they all sat chatting by the pool. Martha raved about the few stores mostly. She showed them an enameled snuffbox from the nineteenth century that she'd bought at one of the antique shops.

"I'll use it to carry aspirins or something. Isn't it dainty? It will remind me of this lovely weekend." She cast a sad smile at Hal.

Since Martha was keeping everyone amused, Sally had time to think. She noticed that at least John wasn't taking pictures, as she'd feared he might. When they went in for lunch, she found a minute to tell Hal that she thought John had been snooping in his room. She and Hal stayed behind to collect the glasses while the others went inside to change.

"I think it's time we flushed them out, before I do something foolish," Hal said.

"Like fall in love with Martha, you mean?" Sally asked warily. She didn't even want to say the words.

"She's a wonderful woman, Sally. So intelligent and well educated."

"She's way too young for you."

"I'm young at heart, my dear. Let me enjoy my declining years in my own way. Martha speaks French and Italian and Spanish. She's cosmopolitan in her outlook. She reminds me of Sophia. Not in looks but in her manner. A man can talk to her about anything—philosophy, politics. You don't find many women that well-rounded at her age."

"Yes, she's the eighth wonder of the world, Hal, but she's also here to steal your novel for Wigo. You're so blinded by her you haven't really done a thing to catch them. I thought the Silver Fox would have come up with a plan before now," she taunted.

"She's wasting her talents with that two-bit agency she works for."

"You said it must be a top-notch agency."

"The work is beneath her. She's wasting her time, and as you so snidely pointed out, I am wasting mine.

I haven't been completely asleep at the switch, how- ever. I mean to have an accident at lunch. Just go along with me. Do what I suggest. *Capice?*"

"I get it. What are you going to do?"

"You'll behave more naturally if you don't know. Your face has a tendency to reveal too much."

They took the tray inside and Sally went upstairs to change. When she returned downstairs, the other were already at the table.

Once again Martha took control of the conversa- tion, praising the simple meal of homemade leek soup and hot buns, cold cuts and an assortment of cheeses as if they were haute cuisine. Sally noticed she did more praising than actual eating, and she had the svelte figure to prove it. All through the meal, Sally was on pins and needles, waiting for Hal's accident. What did he plan to do? Spill the soup? That would hardly catapult Martha into a confession, or prove anything.

She was seized with the idea that he meant to have an imaginary heart attack. He was going to let on he was dying, and try to get Martha to confess. No, that couldn't be it. It was the dying person who made a deathbed confession. Dessert was brought in—a fresh fruit compote with yogurt and little thin gingersnap cookies on the side. She looked expectantly at Hal, who ate unconcernedly.

The meal was over, and still no accident. Mrs. Hudson set a little dish of peppermints on the table when she brought in the coffee. Had Hal told her to spill the coffee? Gee, that could be dangerous. She leaned well away from the pot when Mrs. Hudson poured hers. All the cups were filled, and still no ac- cident.

"Try one of these, Martha," Hal said, passing the peppermints. "I have them imported from Scotland. They're very hot."

Martha took one and found it, of course, delicious. Hal popped one into his mouth before passing the dish along to John. When Hal finally had his accident, he did take Sally by surprise.

"Aaargh!" he moaned and put his napkin to his mouth. From behind it he said, "I've broken a tooth with that hard candy." He probed around with his tongue and said, "My cap's loose. And on a front tooth, too. A blow to my vanity. I really must get to my dentist at once, or I'll be out of commission all weekend. He goes to his cottage on Sunday."

"Let me make the call for you, Hal," Martha said. "Is there anything I can do? A glass of water, an aspirin? Does it hurt very much?"

"You give Philips a buzz, will you, Sal? You know his number. Unfortunately, my dentist is in Guelph," he said to Martha. "I'll have to leave you for an hour or so."

Their dentist was Dr. Hooper, so Sally assumed this was all window dressing. This was the accident she'd been waiting for, and she was to go along with whatever he said.

"Let me drive you, Hal," Martha said. "You may not feel like driving when you leave the dentist's office. It's such an emotional drain."

"It may take an hour or more," Hal said. "I wouldn't want to leave you sitting in the doctor's waiting room on such a fine day. You could always go to my apartment, of course. It's just around the corner.... But no, I've given Mrs. Locum the weekend

off. You'd be all alone. You'd be better entertained
here, having a swim. I'll be back as soon as I can."

"I wouldn't mind waiting. Really, I'd rather be with
you," Martha said eagerly.

Sally was beginning to discern his plan. He was going to let Martha loose in the apartment, believing she
was alone, then come back unexpectedly and catch her
red-handed. What Sally hadn't figured out yet was
Hal's plan for John.

"Can I do anything to help?" John asked. "I could
drive you to Guelph."

"I'll ask Sally to drive me," Hal said. "She's more
familiar with the territory."

"I'll be glad to," Sally said.

"But then we're abandoning our guests," Hal said,
as though trying to think what to do. He rubbed his
mouth and winced so convincingly Sally wasn't sure
he was faking about the tooth. Maybe he had accidentally loosened the cap.

"We can entertain ourselves," Martha said. "Don't
worry about us, Hal. You just do whatever you have
to. I hope it's not too painful."

"It's beginning to throb," he said. "I gave the cap
quite ajar. I've had a root canal, but something's
aching."

Martha sat a moment, thinking. "You know, I
particularly wanted to see that lovely cathedral in
Guelph. The old stone Gothic one that sits on a little
hill, overlooking the town. I could do that while you're
at the dentist's and meet you back at the apartment."

"I don't want to leave John here alone," Hal said.

"Why don't I go along for the ride?" John suggested, not eagerly, but as if he just didn't want to be
any trouble.

Sally glanced at Hal, to see if this was what he wanted. He had told Martha and John that he did all his writing at the apartment. Martha had already searched the office here at the farm, and John had searched the bedroom, so they knew there was nothing to find here. Hal was luring them to the apartment. Sly old Silver Fox! It had to be done, but she wasn't looking forward to the confrontation.

"Can you find something to do in town for an hour or so, John?" Hal asked. "Sally will wait for me at the dentist's."

"I can just walk around, maybe have a look at the university campus. I saw some greenhouses that looked interesting."

"You'll need a car to get there," Hal said. "You could take Sally's and meet us back at the dentist's in an hour. Does that leave everyone with something to do?" he asked, as though his only concern was for his guests' pleasure.

But Sally noticed he had arranged to give John the apartment keys. That key was on the same key chain as her car keys. John and Martha would think they had ample time for a leisurely search of an empty apartment. She'd have to phone Mrs. Locum and ask her to clear out for a couple of hours. Mrs. Locum lived at the apartment, weekends included.

"I'll give you my keys, Martha," Hal said, "so you can let yourself into the apartment when you've had your fill of sight-seeing."

"About an hour, you think you'll be?" Martha asked.

"Not much more than that, I hope. You'd better give Dr. Philips a buzz, Sally, if you don't mind."

She read the message in his look, and went to phone Mrs. Locum. The housekeeper was accustomed to strange requests from her employer.

"I'll just drop in next door and visit the neighbors," the housekeeper said when Sally had explained the situation. "Call me when the coast is clear."

"You're an angel," Sally said.

"Which is more than can be said for you and your uncle. I want a full report when this is over, you hear?"

"You'll get it."

Sally returned to the table and said, "All set, Hal. Dr. Philips is in his office. He'll wait until you get there."

"The sooner, the better," Hal said resignedly, rubbing his mouth. "I don't look forward to this. I'd rather have a major operation than let a dentist at me. At least they give you an anesthetic for an operation."

"Ask the doctor to give you a freezing," Martha said supportively. "I hate to think of you suffering. We'll stay in tonight and let you recuperate."

There had been talk of going to the dance at Hal's golf club.

"We'll see," he said, patting her hand. "I was looking forward to dancing with you."

"We'd better be going," Sally said. "I told the dentist we'd be there as soon as possible. We'll take my car, Hal? Yours doesn't hold four." Hal nodded.

"You'd better keep the top up, Sally," Martha said. "The wind won't do Hal's tooth any good." She turned to Hal. "Why don't you let me put a scarf around your jaw? The warmth will feel good."

"Very thoughtful of you, Martha," Hal said. "I'm sorry to be such a nuisance. Are you sure you wouldn't rather stay here and swim? It's such a fine day."

Sally knew there was no chance of her staying, and so did Hal. Of course Martha insisted on going. She sat in the back seat with Hal, holding his hand and comforting him while Sally drove into Guelph.

"I'll drop you off at the church, Martha," Sally said. "It isn't actually a cathedral, just a big church."

"Fine," Martha nodded. "I'll meet you all back at the apartment around three-thirty."

"Have you got Hal's keys?" Sally asked her.

Martha had already taken care of that important detail.

The Church of Our Lady Immaculate was a landmark in Guelph. It was a good copy of a thirteenth-century French Gothic church. It sat on a hill overlooking the busy downtown heart of the city. Eight different flights of stairs led up to it. It was an impressive sight, with its twin steeples and soaring spires lined against the azure sky. The vestigial flying buttresses and the lancet windows added to its majesty. Martha got out and began the long ascent up the stairs.

Sally drove toward their apartment, since Hal had said his dentist was close to it.

"You remember where the dentist's office is?" Hal said. "In that high-rise office building on the corner a block down from the apartment?"

"I know where you mean," she said. When she reached it, she pulled over to the curb.

"The doctor's office is on the third floor here," Hal said to no one in particular.

Sally said, "I'll just leave the motor running, John. You know how to get to the university?"

"I'll find it."

"You'll have time to tour the campus, but don't get lost in the arboretum again."

"See you in an hour." He turned to Hal. "Good luck with the dentist."

Hal and Sally got out and went into the office building. They watched from the doorway to see where John went. He slid in behind the wheel and disappeared into the traffic.

When he was gone, Hal said, "If he's worth his salt, he'll come back here and check to see there is a Dr. Philips in this building. I made sure to use a real dentist."

"Why didn't you use your own?"

"Because he's in the wrong location. I wanted one close to the apartment, so we can keep an eye on things."

"If you think John will come back here, we'd better hide."

"He may pick up Martha first, since they're working together. We'll give him five minutes to go around the block. If he's not back, we'll assume he's gone after Martha."

They waited five minutes, peering from the doorway. When they saw the little red convertible cruise by, looking for a parking spot, they went into an insurance office on the main floor where they could keep an eye on the lobby without being seen.

It was another few minutes before John strode into the lobby. He went straight to the bulletin board to read the names of the occupants. Apparently he was satisfied that Hal really was with Dr. Philips, because he turned around and left at a fast pace.

"He really should have phoned Dr. Philips," Hal said. "He could have made some excuse. We'll get a cab and cruise by the church. You take a peek in. Make sure Martha doesn't see you, if she's there."

"Which she won't be. I'll put on a kerchief to hide my hair and just peek in the door to check."

The taxis were easy to spot. They were a dull moss green color with yellow and black trim. Hal hailed one and they were off to the church. Hal stayed in the cab while Sally ran up the stairs to the church. She was panting by the time she got to the top. She caught her breath while she put on her kerchief, then went to the door.

A hushed sense of sanctity greeted her when she went inside. The only illumination was the stained-glass windows that cast an eerie light on the nearly empty pews. At the front of the long nave, a majestic white marble altar was bathed in red and blue light from the stained-glass windows. There were two or three dozen people in the church, but it was so big it looked empty. A few people were just looking around, others were kneeling at the altar, and others were lined up at the confessionals. A red plush carpet softened her footfalls as she went forward, peering all around. When Sally was satisfied that Martha wasn't there, she returned to the cab.

"Not a sign of her," she said. "Let's go to the apartment. They're probably rifling it by now."

They had just given the driver instructions when Sally recognized her red convertible cruising by the church. It pulled up in front and parked where it

shouldn't. One other illegally parked car was between
the convertible and the taxi, giving them some cover.

John got out and looked all around, as if looking
for someone, presumably Martha. Then he looked
toward the taxi. They ducked down to hide their
heads. John continued looking at it suspiciously for a
minute. Fortunately a woman wanting a taxi headed
to it, and John was satisfied. He darted up the stairs
and into the church.

"He's looking for Martha," Hal said. "They didn't
have any time to make plans."

Meanwhile the hopeful customer had discovered
them crouching in the back seat and took exception to
it. She was a large, bustling woman with a loud voice
and a querulous temper. "Here, what are you two up
to?" she demanded. "What's going on here? You
ought to be ashamed of yourself. Don't you know this
is a consecrated church?"

Hal looked up and smote her with his most win-
ning smile. "I lost my contact lens," he said. "I'm
most terribly sorry, madam. This cab is taken."

"Aren't you getting out? I saw you drive up. You've
reached your destination, haven't you?"

Sally peered out the window and saw John come
pelting out of the church as if the hounds of hell were
after him. She poked Hal in the ribs and nodded at
John.

They both ducked back down to hide their heads.
"No," Hal said, looking up from the floor. "We just
stopped so I could find my lens."

"I can't imagine why people go sticking lenses in
their eyes. It's dangerous. Here, I'll help you look.
I've got perfect eyesight."

"That isn't necessary," Hal said, his patience wearing thin.

Sally peered out of the window again and saw that John was looking at the cab.

The overbearing woman spoke on. "Where are you going anyway? Maybe I can share your cab. I'm in a hurry."

Hal pulled the door closed in her face and said to the driver, "Get us out of here, fast."

Tires squealed and the cab shot off, away from John. "Where to?" the cabbie asked.

"Follow that red car," Hal said, pointing back to Sally's convertible, that was just moving away from the cathedral.

"I can't do a U-turn in traffic!"

"There's twenty bucks in it for you," Hal said.

"Right you are, pal."

Tires squealed again, and the car turned around, amid an angry honking of horns. They caught up to the convertible at the first traffic light, with a few cars between them.

"Did you find your lens?" the driver asked over the seat.

Hal just rolled his eyes ceilingward and said, "Yes, thank you."

"You shouldn't put it back in until you've cleaned it. You can get an infection that way. You never know what's been going on in the back seat of a cab."

"Thanks for the advice," Hal said. Sally swallowed a smile and peered ahead to keep sight of her car as the light changed and they pulled forward.

"He isn't going to the apartment," she said. "Where's he going? He turned onto the main street."

"Your husband?" the driver asked in a sympathetic way.

Hal said, "Yes," and Sally said, "No!" at the same time.

"Sorry I asked," the cabbie said and gave up on them. A moment later he said, "Your man's stopping. What do you want me to do?"

"Stop as close behind him as you can," Hal said. "What's in that building, do you know?"

"Federal offices. Customs, immigration, RCMP."

"The Mounties?" Hal exclaimed.

"That's right," the cabbie said, eyeing them very much askance. He pulled around the corner and parked. "I don't want no trouble, folks. Maybe you'd better get out. That'll be twenty-seven bucks."

"We're not causing any trouble!" Sally exclaimed.

"Gross impertinence!" Hal said, staring malignly at the man.

The cabbie just went on glaring. "You ought to be ashamed of yourselves. Get out."

"Hal, do something!" Sally said, furious.

Hal handed him a twenty-dollar bill, and added a ten. "Thank you, my good man. Keep the change. I suggest you use it to have the rear of this abominable car cleaned up."

"Thanks. No hard feelings, eh?" the cabbie said.

They got out and he drove away, leaving them on the street corner.

"What did he think we were doing?" Sally asked in confusion.

"God only knows. More important, what is McCallum up to? I think the thing to do, Sally, is you follow him when he leaves, and I'll have a word with the Mounties. I have friends there. If McCallum is trying some con job on them, they'll want to hear about it.''

"How will I follow him?''

"I suggest you run out and hail another cab, Countess, unless you think you can keep up with a car on foot.''

"One of us should go to the apartment and check up on Martha.''

"I expect that's where John will go next. In fact, I'm sure of it. You can just have the cab take you there. We'll meet there. Don't go in alone. I don't think there's any physical danger, but it will be better if you not go in alone.''

"I'll wait next door with Mrs. Locum.''

"Fine. Now run along. Do you have your toy gun? An illusion of firepower might come in handy.''

"Yes, I have it—but John has a real one.''

"I hardly think he's likely to murder you,'' Hal said as he scanned the street for a cab.

One was just passing. The bustling woman from the cathedral sat in it. She stared as if she had seen a ghost and urged the driver on faster. The next one was empty and Sally hopped in. As she drove away, she saw Hal getting a newspaper from a vending machine. He'd use that to cover his face if John came out unexpectedly.

She didn't have to worry about the Silver Fox. He could take care of himself. She wasn't very worried about Martha, either. Her own emotions had less to do with fear than unhappiness.

John had lied to her. He had promised he was quitting the case, but his surreptitious actions made it perfectly clear he hadn't. And once he was caught, the only decent thing he could do was apologize and leave.

She'd never see him again. He'd go on to some other
job, and she'd go to Italy to try to forget. She didn't
have a snuffbox or any memento of the weekend, like
Martha, but she knew she wouldn't soon forget it.

Chapter Nine

At the apartment building, Sally got off the elevator one floor below Hal's apartment and took the stairs up to the penthouse, in case anyone was listening for the elevator. She went to the Cassidys' apartment, across the hall. Mrs. Locum opened the door even before she knocked, and Sally slipped in quietly. The housekeeper had had her eye to the peephole, which gave a perfect view of Hal's door.

"Has anybody gone into the apartment?" Sally asked.

"No, and I haven't removed my eye from this peephole since I got here," Mrs. Locum replied. "Mrs. Cassidy had to go out. I'm minding her sick cat, so we're alone. Now tell me what you and your uncle are up to, missie."

"It's kind of a complicated story," Sally said. Then she told Mrs. Locum the basic outline.

They took turns looking out the hole to watch the door across the hall. After half an hour no one had come, and Sally began to wonder what had gone wrong with the plan. Martha and John both had keys; they knew the apartment was empty, but they didn't come. Did they know it was a setup? What were they doing instead? Most of all, she wondered why John had visited the RCMP.

Of course the Mounties didn't occupy the whole federal building. There were all sorts of other offices there also. Or maybe he knew he was being followed and wanted to throw them off his trail. Hal had said he'd be right back, but he didn't come, either. When the phone rang, Sally jumped a foot, until she remembered it would be for Mrs. Cassidy.

Mrs. Locum answered. "For you, Sally," she called from the kitchen. "It's your uncle. I'll watch the door."

Sally ran and snatched up the phone. "Any action on your end?" Hal asked.

"No, not a sign of them."

"I knew McCallum wouldn't be there. He's gone shopping."

"What!"

"He parked the damned car in the Eaton's garage and went into the shopping mall."

"Maybe he's meeting someone."

"I bought a cap and a black shirt for a disguise. I feel like a hobo. I've been tailing him. At the moment, he's at that big hardware store. He's looking at tennis racquets."

"I don't believe this! He's spotted you, Hal. He's leading you on a merry chase, but why hasn't Martha come?"

"We've goofed up somehow. You stick around for another few minutes, then meet me at the dentist's office. That's where John's picking us up."

"All right," she said, and hung up in confusion.

A little bubble of joy was rising in her. Maybe John really had quit the case! He had still been working on it earlier in the day, when he was in Hal's room, but something must have changed his mind. He had been friendly at the pool. That must be when he decided he couldn't go on lying to her. And he must have convinced Martha to quit, too. Martha seemed to like Hal very much, and if she thought the feeling was reciprocated—well, maybe she'd rather be married to a handsome, successful novelist than work for a detective agency.

The next few minutes seemed an eternity. Sally stared out the peephole until her eyes were watering, praying that John wouldn't come. And he didn't. Neither did Martha. When the quarter of an hour was up, Sally went downstairs and out to walk the half block to the dentist's office.

She met Hal, wearing the cap and shirt and carrying a bag, but he didn't look much like a hobo. The black shirt was of stone-washed silk. They hustled into the building. The lobby was deserted on a Saturday afternoon.

"I don't get it. I just don't get it," he said. "It was a perfect plan. How did it go wrong?" While he spoke, he was pulling off the black shirt and pulling his own shirt out of the bag to change.

"Maybe they've changed their minds, Hal," Sally said hopefully. "I mean Martha seems to like you, and I think John cares for me."

"Spare me," he said, with a withering look. "Your juvenile romantic streak is warping your judgment.

I've warned you of that before. If you had your way, all my books would have happy endings. You'll find, as you grow up, that love affairs seldom have happy endings.''

The virulence of his attack told Sally Hal was emotionally involved himself. "Sounds like an overreaction to me," she said. "Do you have a better explanation?"

"No," he admitted with a smile. "Do you really think—"

"It's possible. Love conquers all, they say."

"It certainly conquers common sense. In any case, we'll carry on as if nothing had happened."

"Nothing did happen," Sally pointed out.

"You know what I mean. We'll go to the dance at the club this evening, but I won't breathe easy until Martha confesses and tells me she's abandoned the case. She owes me that."

"Yeah," Sally agreed. She remembered that John had already told her he'd abandoned the case, and he'd apologized. That seemed to give her the right to admit she loved him.

"We'll wait here in the lobby," Hal said. "I'll rub my mouth a little to make it look as if I've been mauled by the dentist."

"What are you going to do with that shirt?"

"There must be a refuse bin here somewhere."

"Refuse bin! It's silk. If you don't want it, I'll take it." Hal tucked in his shirttails.

"He'll wonder where that bag came from," he said.

"He'll think I slipped out to do a little shopping while you were getting your tooth fixed."

"So he will. It sounds exactly like a woman."

"Better hurry up. John's coming," Sally said, as she spotted him coming through the outer door.

Hal stuffed the shirt and cap into the shopping bag and handed the bag to Sally as John approached.

His brow was furrowed in concern. The convertible left his hair windblown, giving him a boyish look. Sally wanted to run and pitch herself into his arms. When he looked up and saw her, a slow smile moved his lips. It rose to his blue eyes, that glowed in pleasure. He remembered his manners, and asked Hal how he felt, before speaking to Sally.

"I'm fine," Hal said, with the kind of smile a man wears when he's leaving the dentist—or when he's in love. "All it took was a daub of cement, or whatever it is they use to hold on the cap. Philips told me not to eat or drink anything hot for a couple of hours. That seems to leave me no choice but a glass of whiskey to calm my nerves. Shall we go and meet Martha?"

"The car's right outside," John said. His eyes just skimmed off the bag Sally was carrying. "I'm glad everything went well, Hal."

"I never felt better," Hal smiled. "This hard-hearted niece of mine deserted me and went shopping." He got into the back seat to let Sally sit with John in front.

"You know what they say," Sally grinned. "When the going gets tough, the tough go shopping."

"Do you want to drive?" John asked her.

"You go ahead. What did you do while we were at the dentist's, John? Did you take a tour of the campus?"

"No, I decided to have a look at that church. Very handsome. I got detoured at the mall. Nearly bought a tennis racquet, but they're cheaper at home. All those Canadian taxes!" As she spoke, he pulled into the traffic.

"Tell me about it," Sally groaned. She noticed that John gave a truthful account of his afternoon, only leaving out his stop at the federal building.

"I think we should stay in town tonight and celebrate Hal's safe deliverance from the dentist," John suggested. "My treat. Let me take us all out to dinner."

"Mrs. Hudson would take that amiss," Hal said. "She's preparing her specialty—coq au vin. And I promised Martha we'd go dancing tonight at my club in Georgetown. We hoped you and Sally would join us."

"That sounds great," John said. "You certainly entertain your guests royally, Hal."

"You have to make your own entertainment in these small towns. Now if we were in Paris or London or Rome—"

They were at the apartment before he could begin on the delights of European capitals. John parked in the apartment garage and they went up to the penthouse.

"Martha will let us in," Hal said, tapping on the door. There was no answer. "She's still out raiding the shops, I expect. Unfortunately, she has my key."

"My key's on that ring," Sally mentioned to John, and he let them in, then gave her back her keys.

All three looked around expectantly. Hal went to the kitchen to get ice for the drinks, taking a look in his bedroom cum office on the way. Sally could see the computer room was empty. Martha wasn't here.

Hal made himself a stiff drink and got beer for the others. Conversation was easy. Hal mostly talked about golf. He was trying to lower his handicap. Since neither John nor Sally played golf, they just listened.

Hal hoped to have a game with Martha tomorrow at his club.

They were half finished their drinks when an apologetic Martha arrived, loaded down with bags and boxes.

"I'm so sorry I'm late," she said, and went to give Hal a kiss on the cheek. "How did it go with the dentist? Not too bad, I hope."

"Piece of cake," Hal said, using the phrase that he so often chided his niece for using. "We're celebrating my deliverance with a drink. You must drink to my tooth."

"I'd love a cup of tea," she said. "Would it be too much trouble, Sally? I'll help myself if—"

"No trouble," Sally said and went to make the tea. She hoped John might join her, but he didn't.

While she was waiting for the water to boil, she phoned Mrs. Locum from the kitchen and told her she could come back as soon as they left. "A false alarm," she said, laughing for joy. "I'll give you all the details on Monday."

"You people are nuts," Mrs. Locum said.

Since Sally would be driving back to the farm, she didn't have another drink, but Hal was so happy he had a second one to keep Martha company with her tea. Martha confessed, with a girlish grin, that she hadn't stayed long at the church. She was overcome with an urge to go shopping. Sally felt for the first time that she could come to like Martha. They soon went to the car and drove to Hilltop.

There was a festive air on the drive that really had very little to do with Hal's safe deliverance from the dentist. Sally was looking forward to the dance. The country club was a much classier place than the Club 2000. It definitely called for a fancy dress. The music was more old-fashioned. The band played some modern pieces for the younger club members, but they played older music, too, the kind of music where your partner holds you in his arms. She'd never danced with John like that.

Hal decided he had to have a swim when they got back to the farm. Sally thought he probably just wanted to see Martha in a bathing suit. She was quite a sight. Not a milligram of cellulite anywhere. She wore a svelte one-piece black suit that plunged low in front and very high at the hips. A bracelet would have spanned her tiny waist. She didn't go into the water, but she looked extremely decorative in the lounge chair, cheering Hal on. Sally took it as a major compliment that John didn't drool.

He seemed more interested in Sally. They took Shep for a walk down the road to the Cedarvale Park and watched some kids playing soccer. When Shep decided he wanted to play, they left and took the trail through a sort of mini-wilderness. When they got tired, they sat at one of the picnic tables in the shade and just talked, while the sun sank lower in the west. It fuzzed the treetops with a shimmering copper halo, that John told her looked like her hair.

Neither of them mentioned his working for Wigo. Since he had given up the job, Sally wasn't eager to bring it up. She didn't want to tell him yet about the trick she and Hal had tried to play on him. She'd make her confession later. These private moments were too precious to squander. John talked about his family— he had two sisters, one married and one at college. Sally told him about her childhood, which had been happy but fairly uneventful, except for coming down with tonsillitis and missing her own graduation dance.

"I bet you would have been queen of the ball, too," he said.

"I doubt it, but I had a new dress that I really wanted to show off. I never did get to wear it. I didn't go to many formal affairs, and by the time I got to university, it was out of style."

"You can pack it away with your bikini. Why didn't you wear it? I was looking forward to it."

"I decided it was too risqué."

"Afraid I'd lose control, you mean?" he said, chewing a smile. "You might be right. I'm finding it pretty hard to control myself right now." His eyes gazed at her lips.

Shep barked at him. "Good dog," John said, stroking his ears. "I hope you're equally fierce with all her boyfriends."

"I think he's just hungry," Sally said. "We should be getting back."

They strolled home hand in hand, just in time to change for dinner. Sally wanted to look especially good and wore a romantic flowered dress that sat low on her shoulders and flared in a full skirt below. The green of the pattern picked up the green of her eyes. She scooped her hair back, pinned with a big white silk flower. She knew Martha would wear something sinfully sophisticated and look totally glamorous, but she wasn't competing with Martha. Sophistication wasn't her style, and she didn't think it was John's, either. It was nice to be herself again, all pretenses dropped.

Sally was right about Martha. She wore a drop-dead white dress that clung to her lithe body like Saran Wrap. Her jet hair hung loose in a shiny curtain. Hal wore a white evening jacket. He always wore that to the country club. The two of them looked like fashion models.

John wore a seersucker suit and told Sally he felt like a hick beside the rest of them.

"You look fine to me," she said, putting her hand in his to lead him to the table.

Mrs. Hudson had outdone herself. She not only made her coq au vin, she began the meal with a seafood terrine, bubbling in brandy and bouillon and spiced with a bouquet garni.

"I simply must have this recipe!" Martha exclaimed. "I haven't tasted food like this since the last time I was in Paris."

"I have a little confession," Hal said. "I bribed the chef at Maxim's with an autographed copy of my latest novel, and he gave me the recipe. Fresh spices and good brandy are the secret. It doesn't do the food justice to use inferior brandy or wine."

The coq au vin was Mrs. Hudson's recipe and equally delicious. She served it with a garden salad and hot flaky rolls. A chocolate mousse, light as air and rich as Devon cream, was dessert.

"And no peppermints!" Martha decreed. "I don't want to miss that dance. It's been such a lovely weekend," she said, rather sadly.

"Then you must come back again soon," Hal said.

Sally noticed their hands had disappeared under the table. She'd never seen Hal so smitten before. He was acting like a teenager with his first crush, holding hands under the table. They took their coffee on the patio, to enjoy the last of the sunset. A gentle breeze blew in from the meadow, rippling the long grass and swaying tree branches.

John didn't say much. He was profoundly unhappy, although he tried not to show it. Why couldn't the Silver Fox be satisfied with what he had? He had so much. John liked Hal, but that wasn't the bigger problem. He had found himself liking the people he had to arrest before now. They were frequently charming. What bothered him was what Sally would do when she learned the truth.

He knew she had come to trust him. She had stopped her little seductress act. He liked her much better as herself. He really didn't believe she had a clue what her uncle was up to, and he meant to protect her as much as possible. But even that wouldn't make her forgive him. She'd see the arrest as a betrayal. And she'd see her uncle's behavior as a betrayal. A double betrayal—that was a lot for a young girl to cope with. She wouldn't like him calling her a girl, but that was how he thought of her.

"What are you smirking about?" she asked.

"Am I smirking?" he asked, shaking himself to attention. "I don't know. I guess I was just thinking about that bikini."

"Since it seems to be preying on your mind, I'll model it for you tomorrow, but I don't think it'll live up to your expectations."

"We'll see about that," he said, and swallowed the deep sigh that rose up inside him. By tomorrow she'd know the truth. And by tomorrow evening at this time he'd be out of her life, on his way back to Washington. He never would get to see that bikini.

"Are you folks about ready to roll?" Hal asked.

"I just want to freshen my makeup," Martha said, heading up to her room.

Sally went to the kitchen for a moment to congratulate Mrs. Hudson.

"I'm glad you liked it, Sally. The mousse turned out well, if I do say so myself. I've just left the champagne in the fridge to cool. I'll put out the glasses, and

Mr. Harmon can do the honors. I'll be gone before you get back.''

"Champagne, eh? I didn't know Hal planned to serve champagne after the dance.''

"Oh, he didn't buy it. It was that nice Mr. McCallum. He bought it while you were all in Guelph this afternoon and sneaked it in as a surprise. He said not to tell Mr. Harmon, but I thought you probably knew about it.''

"No, I didn't, but I won't let on I know.'' That was a nice gesture on John's part.

"Have a good time at the dance.''

"I intend to. And thanks again for that lovely dinner.''

They all met back in the living room. "You'll take your own car, Sally?'' Hal said, which meant he wanted to be alone with Martha.

"Sure, Hal. We'll see you there.'' Hal and Martha left first.

"We'll leave the top of the convertible up, to protect my hair,'' Sally said. "Not that the wind would harm it, but this flower might decide to leave.''

"That flower's half as big as your head,'' John joked, touching it as an excuse to run his fingers through her hair.

"Don't you like it?'' she asked. "I can take it off if—''

"It looks fine. That wasn't a complaint. Quite the contrary. You look perfect.''

"Then why do you look so sad?'' she asked.

"I was just thinking of that graduation dance you missed,'' he said in a gentle voice. "I wish I could make it up to you.''

"You already have," she said as she put her small hand trustingly in his. "We'll call this my graduation dance, okay?"

"I should have gotten you a corsage."

She patted the big flower on her head. "I already have one. Let's go."

The clubhouse was only a mile away. It was a low, sprawling building surrounded by the undulating greens of the golf course. A few people were playing tennis on the lighted courts outside. John stopped a moment to watch them.

"We can play tomorrow while Hal and Martha golf, if you like," Sally said. "I'm not very good, but I do have a racquet. You could use Hal's."

"Great," he said, forcing a note of enthusiasm. That was something else he would have enjoyed but would never do with Sally.

They went into the dim dance hall. The place was rapidly filling up. A small band played the sort of music that, in theory, appealed to all ages, but the couples on the dance floor were mostly over forty. Heads turned to stare at Martha and Hal. A few people knew him by name and shouted greetings. They found a table and Hal ordered drinks.

"I'm in the mood for a tango," Hal said. "Do you tango, Martha?"

"Yes, but isn't it rather—I mean, you don't see many people tango these days."

"It's an art form," Hal said. "I've seen it performed in Argentina, where it comes from. Tango means 'I touch.' The bodies caress. Come, let's show them how it's done," he said, and took her with him to talk to the orchestra.

As soon as the last piece finished, the band began a tango. A few couples remained on the floor but soon edged to the side, leaving Hal to show them how it was done. He was certainly a good dancer, and Martha kept pace with him. The music had almost a militaristic beat to it. It seemed less a dance of love than a contest, despite the provocative body postures.

"I think Hal's really falling for Martha," Sally said.

"I think it cuts both ways," John replied.

"It's funny, isn't it?" she said pensively. "You and Martha came here to—you know—rip Hal off, and instead you both fell—I mean Martha fell in love with Hal," she finished lamely. She was hot and blushing furiously. She had nearly said John had fallen in love with her, too. She felt in her bones he had, but since he hadn't said so, she didn't want to say it.

"You were right the first time," he said with a knowing smile. "We both fell head over heels in love with our intended victims."

The words flowed through her like champagne, warming and exhilarating and making her dizzy with joy. She didn't say anything. She didn't have to. John could see the effect of his declaration. She wouldn't be glowing like a thousand-watt bulb if she didn't feel the same way. He shouldn't have told her. The least painful thing he could do would be to change the subject.

He said, "How did you find out about Martha working for Wigo?"

Sally seemed reluctant to switch subjects, but she answered politely. "We've known for ages. Hal saw you go into her room that night at your hotel. Two nights ago, was it? It seems ages."

"Has Hal spoken to her about it?"

"No, he's hoping she confesses. Do you think she will?"

"I urged her to forget the whole thing. She said she would. I figured when she didn't make use of her opportunity this afternoon, she wasn't going to. Hal set her up?"

"Yes," she admitted.

"I wondered at the Fox being so careless about the apartment. I should have known. I wouldn't have let her get away with it, of course."

Sally didn't say anything, but the love and admiration in her eyes made him feel ten feet tall.

At the end of the tango, Hal and Martha were invited to a friend's table. The band played a slow number, and John and Sally danced. He held her close. The difference in their heights left his chin touching the top of her head. He wished he could steal a kiss. Knowing that Sally really cared for him, it seemed cruel to lead her on, though. It was a bittersweet dance. His whole body responded to hers. It promised so much, but by tomorrow she'd despise him.

John tried to keep up a show of spirits. As the evening wore on the band played more music for the younger couples, the kind of music where you couldn't hold your date in your arms. And maybe that was just as well.

By midnight, everyone was tired from a full day. It was Martha who suggested they leave. Sally noticed that, although Martha's lips were smiling, her eyes held that same rather sad expression as John's. She gazed at Hal as if she were storing up memories for future repining. She was probably afraid Hal would blow a fuse when she confessed to working for Wigo.

Maybe John's champagne would cheer Martha up, and if it didn't, Hal's proposal would. Sally felt in her bones Hal was going to propose to her. It would please his vanity that he had won over the woman who had come to harm him. That story would feature in their future life together.

They all met back at the farm. "Now for a night-cap," Hal announced.

"Let me take care of it, Hal," John said as he went to the kitchen. Sally let him go alone and prepared an expression of surprised delight when he brought in the champagne.

He had brought two bottles and extravagantly opened both of them. "Maybe you should save one for tomorrow," Sally said when he began to uncork the second. "We've already had a few drinks. We'll never be able to drink two bottles."

"This is a two-bottle night," John insisted, and handed her a glass, then poured one for Hal. She noticed that he poured his own and Martha's wine from the other bottle. It was done casually. He set the first bottle down and nonchalantly picked up the other bottle, as if by chance. Now why had he done that? Hal proposed a toast.

"To new friends," he said. "May they become, in the fullness of time, old and dear friends."

"I'll drink to that," Martha said, gazing deeply into his eyes.

Sally sipped her champagne. It tasted fine. She had seen John open the bottles herself, so there was no way he could have tampered with them. She was ready to forget it, until she noticed Hal slip the metal paper from one bottle into his pocket, while John was putting the bottles back into the ice bucket.

What was Hal looking for? The tops hadn't been tampered with, had they? No, it would be impossible to get the paper off and the cork out without leaving any sign. But maybe— A needle with a syringe attached, pushed through the paper and cork wouldn't leave much of a mark. Just a needle prick. That's what Hal was looking for! And if he found it, then that meant John had doctored the wine. He was trying to poison them, or at least put them to sleep while he carried on with his job. The job he'd promised her he had given up.

And Martha was in on it with him. He'd served her from the same bottle he used for himself. Sally wandered off to the corner and tipped her drink into a rubber plant, then returned. John filled her glass and smiled. "Don't drink too fast, now. I don't want to get you tipsy."

"It's delicious," she said.

Martha strolled over to admire a flower painting, and the others went with her. Sally picked up the other foil wrapping and went into the kitchen. She held it up to the light and saw a pinhole. So that was what John was up to.

She took the paper and put it back where John had left it. Then she joined the others. She noticed Hal's glass was empty too, but she doubted very much that he'd drunk the wine.

"You need a refill, Hal," she said. "John, would you do the honors?"

John took the glass, and Martha wandered off to look out the window. Sally said in a low voice to Hal, "I checked the other foil paper. It's the one he doctored. Don't drink that champagne."

"Don't worry, Countess, I didn't come down in the last rain. I just hope it doesn't kill my plants. Mrs. Hudson loves those plants."

When John gave him another glass, he lifted it to his lips and pretended to drink. "Ah, there's nothing like champagne," he said. "The trouble with French champagne is that it goes down so easily. This is excellent stuff, John. I have a fondness for Veuve Clicquot myself. You didn't buy this in Georgetown! They have a very limited selection of champagne.''

"No, I picked it up in Guelph.''

"Extravagant. You really shouldn't have.''

"You've given us such a delightful weekend, I wanted to show my appreciation.''

"It was very kind of you. I think I'll rustle up a plate of crackers and cheese. I always like to nibble a little something with wine.''

Hal went to the kitchen, and when he returned, his glass was empty. "You didn't put on any of the Brie, Hal,'' Sally said. "I'll get it.'' She went and poured her wine down the sink, got the Brie and returned.

She noticed John had filled his own and Martha's glass again from the undoctored bottle. She figured two glasses were enough to make her sleepy and began yawning.

"I think I'm ready for bed,'' she said. She wasn't imagining that quick exchange of looks between John and Martha, or the satisfied little smile that John wore.

"It's been a long day,'' Hal said, also rising. "And a perfectly lovely one, barring that trip to the dentist.''

John held up the doctored bottle. "There's still some wine left,'' he tempted.

"Seems a shame to waste it,'' Hal said, and held out his glass. "I'll take a glass to bed with me. I like to read a few pages of the classics in bed before sleeping. I'm working my way through Montaigne at the moment. In French, of course. I'll just lock up before I go.''

"I'll take care of that, Hal,'' John offered. He could hardly damp down the curiosity as he examined Hal for signs of sleepiness.

"Don't worry about the mess," Hal said. "Mrs. Hudson comes early in the morning. If you'd just put the cheese back in the fridge, Sally." He shook his head wearily. "I don't know what's come over me. The aftermath of the dentist, I guess. I feel fatigued."

"I'll do it," Martha said. "You look sleepy, too, Sally. Don't worry, John and I will take care of things down here." She went to the bottom of the stairs with Hal.

John said to Sally, "I can't tell you how much this weekend has meant to me." He wanted to say more—that he was sorry she had got caught up in this, he had to do his job.

"Me, too," she said, willing a smile onto her face. "I'll see you tomorrow. We'll get up early and grab a court right after breakfast."

"I'm looking forward to it. Sleep tight." He bent down and kissed her, just a light touch on the lips.

She left, before the tears spurted. Hal had already gone upstairs, but Martha was still in the darkened hallway. Sally thought she saw a glitter of tears at her eyes. "Good night, Martha."

"Good night, Sally."

Sally went straight to Hal's room and tapped lightly at the door. He opened it at once and drew her in. "We've got to talk!" he said.

Chapter Ten

Sally noticed that her uncle was looking old, all of a sudden. He had seemed even more dashing and handsome than usual all this weekend. Just a few hours before, club members' heads had turned to stare at him in admiration. Falling in love had made him young again, but disillusionment had reversed the process. His head and shoulders drooped.

"I've been an old fool," he said. "Martha doesn't love me. It was all a con, the oldest trick in the book, and I fell for it."

"I think she does love you, Hal," Sally said. "There were tears in her eyes when I passed her downstairs just now."

A spark of anger flared. "I don't call it love when she's willing to put her job ahead of me. A job such as this one she and McCallum are on, I mean. It's not as though it were a matter of national defense. They're not saving lives, or countries. They're thieves, that's all. And we're going to catch them, Countess.''

"You bet, Dirk," she said gruffly. She knew exactly how Hal felt, because she felt the same herself. She let her anger flare, to keep sorrow at bay. John had betrayed her. He had used her love as a tool against her, and that was the greatest betrayal of all.

This was why Hal's books all had that strain of cynicism. Because he was older and wiser, and knew that men—and women, too—were capable of this base behavior. And it was why she could never like his books as much as she felt she should.

"So, what do we do?" she asked, plopping onto the end of his bed. Hal would have to handle this one, because her brain had just gone on strike. It refused to think about outwitting the enemy, about getting even. What she really wanted to do was go to bed and cry.

"The next move's up to them," Hal said. He was slipping back into his role of the Silver Fox. His shoulders were straighter, his manner cool and determined. "They're after the imaginary Japanese novel, since I convinced them the one they stole is garbage. They think we're sawing logs. Of course they'll come to check, so we'll have to fake it. As soon as they're sure we're asleep, they'll make their move. And we'll follow them. Better hop into bed now, Countess. You needn't bother to undress. Just pull the sheet up over you. It'll save time."

"Right."

She went to her room, kicked off her shoes and got into bed. She lay in the darkness, listening for the tell-tale echo of footsteps on the stairs. The third stair from the top squawked. That would alert her. She never did hear the squawk and was surprised when her

door opened softly. They *were* good! They had noticed that squeaking step, and avoided it.

Her door eased open. Was it Martha or John who
was tiptoeing toward the bed? She peered through her
lowered lashes but could only see a shadow looming
against the dim light from the hallway. When the person—John or Martha—leaned over the bed, her heart
began to bang against her ribs.

They didn't plan to hurt her, did they? Surely they
were just checking to make sure she was asleep. A
hand came out and pulled the sheet back. Oh lord, she
should have gotten undressed! She didn't think they'd
be this thorough. But she was supposed to have been
drugged, so maybe that would explain the dress, if
they could even distinguish it from a nightie in the
darkness.

A hand came out and felt the material of her gown.
She knew, suddenly, that it was John who stood by her
bed. Some instinctive knowledge told her. Maybe it
was a subliminal scent that she picked up, too weak to
actually smell, but enough to tell her. Or maybe a
person has a sixth sense where the one she loves is
concerned. She only knew that John was hovering
over her, gazing down at her. If he didn't leave soon
she'd blow it. Every nerve was wound tight, screaming for release.

The sheet was pulled back up over her shoulders. He
bent toward her as she lay, breath suspended. What
was he doing? Was he going to strangle her? Should
she scream for help or try to escape? Couldn't he hear
the banging of her heart? When she felt she could take
no more, his head suddenly lowered to hers. There was
a warm breath on her cheek. His hand came out and
touched it gently, then moved to stroke her hair. She
bit back an agonizing groan. Whatever John was up

to, he did care for her. She could feel his love surround her in the hushed room. When she felt a fleeting kiss brush her lips, her arms stirred compulsively with the need to hold him.

"I'm sorry, darling," he whispered softly, with infinite regret. That was all he said, then he turned and left, softly closing the door behind him. When she was alone, Sally felt a warm trickle of tears oozing out of her eyes.

Sure he was sorry—but not sorry enough to keep his promise. He was trying to steal Hal's Japanese manuscript and probably get a big fat bonus from Wigo. The ultimate irony was that no such manuscript even existed. She lay still, listening. After two minutes that seemed an hour, the door opened and Hal whispered.

"Get up, Countess. The game's afoot. They've gone downstairs."

She leaped out of bed and scrambled into her shoes, choosing flat heels that would let her run, if running was necessary, and grabbed up her purse.

"What are they doing?" she whispered.

"They went outdoors. I expect the destination is Guelph. My apartment and the Japanese manuscript they fondly imagine is there."

"Then they'll be stealing one of our cars. We can call in the cops."

"We could, but I have a mind to handle this little job personally."

"With the help of Countess Sophia, I hope?"

"That goes without saying."

They crept downstairs in the darkness, out the back door and around to the front, to hide behind the lilac bushes. John had unlocked Sally's convertible and was getting in.

"How did he do that?" she demanded. "He gave my keys back to me." She rooted in her purse and felt her key ring. The other set was in her bedroom in the apartment in Guelph, and John hadn't been near that room.

"That's what he was doing at the hardware store!" Hal exclaimed softly. "He was having your keys copied. He was just looking at the tennis racquet to kill time—or to fool me. This pair is good. I wouldn't be surprised if he'd spotted me following him."

"We'll give them a head start and tail them in your car."

Sally was watching for the headlights to turn down the road out of Hilltop. John didn't use the lights until he was on the road. Sally and Hal hopped into the Porsche and followed them.

"With so little traffic at night, we'd be spotted too easily if we follow them directly," Hal said. "There's not much doubt where they're heading. We'll take another route to the apartment. It's a little longer, but we can drive faster. We'll have a surprise party waiting for them when they arrive."

Sally had engaged in similar escapades with her uncle in the past and had always enjoyed them immensely. But tonight her heart felt like a rock in her chest. The excitement, the thrill, were gone. Hal's powerful car dashed through the night at a speed several miles higher than the legal limit. He was an excellent driver, and there was virtually no traffic on the road at that hour.

Hal babbled on about their making it easy for him. Breaking and entering—maybe he would call the police. The publicity wouldn't do Hugo VanAark any harm.

"You can't buy that kind of advertising," he said. "A story like this makes the front page, not just the book reviews. Of course I'd want to keep my real name out of it."

"I thought you loved Martha!" she said. "Don't you feel sorry at all about what she and John are doing?"

Hal turned a cynical smile on her. "You've heard of sour grapes, Countess, pretending you don't want what you can't have? This is sweet lemons, pretending you like what you're stuck with. Of course I'm sorry that Martha betrayed me, but that doesn't prevent me from seeing the advantages in it. We must play the hand life deals us. And revenge is sweet," he added grimly.

He was being Dirk, and Sally wished she could find a little veneer of sophistication to put over her pain, but she couldn't. There were no aces in the hand fate had dealt her. John had lied to her; he put his job ahead of her. And his job was a tawdry one. He was just a hired thief.

She wasn't at all eager to reach Guelph, but at the speed Hal was driving, they were there in no time. He stopped half a block from the apartment and they got out.

"No lights at the apartment yet," he said, looking up to the top floor of the building. "They'll use the parking garage entrance. We'd better use the front door. I'll tell the doorman not to say we've come, if by any chance Martha uses the front entrance."

How could he think of all these ruses, when his heart was breaking? Sally could only conclude he didn't feel about Martha the way she felt about John. Revenge wasn't going to be sweet for her. It was going to be unbearably bitter. She didn't even want to be there to see John humiliated, taken away by the police, maybe with his wrists in handcuffs. But Hal might need her. She couldn't desert him at this crucial moment.

They left the car where it was and walked to the building. The night watchman was snoozing softly. He was an older man, and nights were usually quiet. It was hard for him to stay awake. They didn't bother waking him.

"We'll let him sleep," Hal said. "He'd be awake if he'd just seen John and Martha coming in. If they came this way, he didn't see it."

They took the elevator to the floor below the top level and walked the last flight, as Sally had done that afternoon. When they reached the hallway to their door, they walked quickly to Hal's apartment. He already had his key out.

"We've beat them," he said. "I'm just wondering if I shouldn't let them go in first. This way, I have no hard evidence. Yes, I think we'll go back to the stairs and wait."

They went back and waited at the top of the stairs, with the door open a crack to see when John and Martha got off the elevator. Five minutes passed, ten. The elevator began to rumble. They listened as it rose higher, but it stopped a few floors below them. No one entered the stairwell. A false alarm.

"What the hell's keeping them?" Hal exclaimed. "We took the long road. They should be here by now."

"Unless he's had an accident!" Sally said.

"The insurance will cover it," Hal said, to comfort her.

It wasn't her car she was worried about. She pictured John, his head bleeding, maybe even dead. "I think we should drive out Highway 7 and have a look, Hal. They might be hurt."

"Is it possible they're not coming here?" he said, rubbing his chin. "They fooled us once before. Where else could they be going?"

"They must have been coming here. They've had an accident."

"I'll call the provincial police from the apartment. That's the fastest way to find out."

They went down the hall toward the apartment. At the door, Hal stopped. He pointed to the peephole. A dim light showed through it.

"There are lights on in there! They beat us. He must have driven like a maniac. Dammit, they've had a quarter of an hour to root. They must have been on their way up when we arrived."

"What are you going to do?"

He drew a gun out of his belt and gave a tight smile. "I'll just have a word with them," he said.

She grabbed his arm. "Hal, remember John has a gun, too."

"A Mexican standoff."

"Call the night security. Harkins has a gun."

Even as they were speaking, the elevator rumbled up to the top floor and opened. The night watchman hurried toward them.

"Mr. Harmon! I saw your car out front. I didn't see you arrive. I must have dozed off," Harkins said apologetically. "You won't tell anyone." He spotted Hal's gun and looked at him.

"No harm done, Harkins. I seem to have intruders," Hal said. "I was just going to call you. You can back me up, if needed."

Harkins was eager to oblige, after having been caught napping. "It's your art they'd be after. I worry about having such valuable paintings in your apartment." The watchman drew his gun. "Let me go first, sir."

"That won't be necessary," Hal smiled. "I don't think it's art thieves. In fact, I doubt there will be gunfire, but a show of strength will intimidate them."

He slid his key in the lock and opened the door quietly. The apartment was blazing with lights in every room. Mrs. Locum came rushing forward with her hair all messy and a dressing gown hastily thrown over her nightgown.

"I didn't mean to do it, Mr. Harmon," she said. "When I heard noises in the living room, I just took up the hammer to protect myself. He had a flashlight and was looking at your paintings."

Over Mrs. Locum's shoulder, Sally saw a strange man, but he didn't look like a burglar. He was well-groomed, wearing a suit and looked like a respectable middle-aged businessman. Were John and Martha part of a bigger gang? Was it the paintings they had been after all the time? Sally looked around for John, but she didn't see him.

Hal seemed to recognize the man in the suit. "Mr. Holden, isn't it?" he said. He slid his gun back into his belt. Then he turned to the night watchman. "It's all right, Harkins. You can leave us. Thanks for your help."

"You're sure?" Harkins asked.

"Quite sure, thanks. Mr. Holden is an old, uh, acquaintance of mind."

Harkins left, but he didn't look too happy about it. Sally figured he'd be waiting right outside the door. Mrs. Locum turned to Sally. "They claim they're Mounties," she said.

"Mounties!"

"They have badges and identification."

"They? Are there more of them?"

"There's one in the kitchen. They said they were Mounties. How was I supposed to know that? I put an ice pack on his head when he came to—the one I hit with the hammer. He doesn't seem to be delirious, but he's awfully angry."

"They're not Mounties," Sally said. Then she began to wonder. Hal didn't seem to be frightened, or even wary, as he would be if he had recognized the man as an art thief. He had put his gun away. While these thoughts flitted through her mind, she looked around for John again. Where was he?

Mrs. Locum said, "I'd better see to my patient." Then she went back to the kitchen.

Sally went to her uncle and tugged at his elbow. "Hal, who is this man?"

"This is Officer Holden, of the RCMP. I am beginning to understand what's going on here now. You recall McCallum paid a call at the federal building this afternoon, well that's when this raid was set up. Right, Holden?"

Officer Holden stood like a statue, not agreeing or disagreeing. After careful consideration he said, "McCallum's in charge."

"And where might I find the elusive John Mc-Callum?" Hal asked.

The Mountie said, "I suggest you and the young lady take a seat. And don't try anything, Harmon. You're not out of the woods yet."

"I hadn't realized I was in the woods. May I have a drink of my own excellent whiskey, or would that be against the law?"

"Feel free," Holden replied. "But don't try anything. You'd better give me your gun."

Hal handed it over. "I have a licence for it. It's loaded, so be careful."

Holden took it and stood with the gun in his hand, not exactly pointed at Hal but ready to be pointed at the first sign of trickery.

Sally said to the officer, "Where's John?"

"He's performing his duty, miss. He'll join us shortly."

"Is he here, in the apartment?"

Holden resumed his granite pose.

"He's in my office, searching my private papers," Hal told her. He had poured himself a drink and sipped it, while a cynical smile curved his lips.

Sally felt a smile pull at her own lips. McCallum is in charge, the Mountie had said. A private investigator for Wigo certainly wasn't in charge, of anything.

"John isn't a private detective, is he, Hal?" she said.

"Brilliant deduction, Countess. It seems our houseguests are CIA. I'd begun to suspect, of course. Martha's credentials were really too good for a private-detective agency. But then she had stolen my novel and was so keenly interested in the Japanese one. When you told me Martha was crying, I felt fairly sure how things stood. She would never choose Wigo over me, but of course being with CIA, her duties took precedence over everything else. I can sympathize with that. Well, they won't find anything. I'm clean."

"I don't even know what they suspect you of," she said.

"Spying, of course. What I wonder is how they ever discovered I'm living in Canada." He looked at Holden. "I rather think that's where the leak came from—the RCMP. My agreement with Scofield was that I keep my nose clean, and they keep their mouths shut."

"Should have kept your nose clean then, Harmon," Holden said.

"I did! I kept my agreement."

"You wrote a letter to a Mr. Ranji."

"About background for my book! Good lord, you can't think Ranji is crooked. Do you mean the Mounties are monitoring my private mail?"

"Standard operational procedure."

"Yes, for suspect characters. I might have known."

There was some noise in the hallway. Soon John and Martha appeared at the doorway of Hal's office. John looked at Sally for a long moment. He didn't say anything, but he looked very upset. Almost frightened.

He turned to Holden. "Everything seems to be kosher," he said. "We found the Ranji correspondence. No secret code there, and Ranji left the country without contacting any known spies."

Hal sat, just smiling cynically. "Do you really think I'd leave incriminating letters sitting around my office?" he asked, and laughed.

"We're just doing our job, Mr. Harmon," John said. "We were told to check you out. Pretty suspicious, you letting on you were dead."

"Only to be spared such annoyances as this, Mc-Callum."

Martha came forward uncertainly and sat down. "I'm sorry, Hal. You know the code. I had to do my job."

Hal patted her hand. "And you did it superbly, my dear."

"Not well enough, I'm afraid. The plan was for us to search your apartment tonight and be back at Hilltop by morning, without your knowing we'd been here. I was sure we wouldn't find anything, but we had to look."

Hal said, "And did you follow *all* the company rules? Keep a cool head, avoid emotional involvement..."

She just looked, while a flush rose up her neck to brighten her cheeks. "I tried," she said softly.

John was acutely aware that Sally was looking at him while that conversation went forth. Her intent gaze seemed to be asking him the same question.

He said, "Maybe you'd have a look at Officer Bertram, Miss Glover. He has a pretty good bump on the head. We didn't realize there was anyone in the apartment. I'm afraid we gave Mrs. Locum quite a scare, arriving in the middle of the night."

Miss Glover! How dare he call her Miss Glover, as if they were strangers. "I'm not a doctor," Sally said. "I wouldn't know if he's badly hurt."

"But maybe you could have a look," he repeated.

"Very well, Mr. McCallum," she said stiffly.

When she went to the kitchen, John followed her. As soon as they were beyond earshot of the other he said, "Sally, I'm sorry. What Martha just said—it goes double for me. I was just doing my job."

"You lied to me. And drugged me."

"I did lie to you, but it seems you outwitted me on the doctored wine. How'd you find out?"

"That needle in the cork trick is so old it has a beard," she scoffed.

A stout man with graying hair sat at the kitchen table with an ice pack held against his forehead. He was sipping coffee and scolding Mrs. Locum.

"A hammer, ma'am. That's undue force. You're only allowed by law to use sufficient force to subdue an intruder. You can't kill him."

"I didn't figure my slipper was sufficient force to subdue a big man like you," Mrs. Locum said. "You've no right to come into people's houses like thieves in the night."

"You weren't supposed to be here. Our information was that the apartment would be empty."

"Next time you'd better check your information."

Sally said to John, "I'd say Officer Bertram is doing just fine, Mr. McCallum."

Mrs. Locum said, "I've made a pot of coffee, if you folks would like some, Sally."

"How long do we have to stay here?" Sally asked John. "Are we under arrest or anything?"

"Of course not."

"Good, then I'll call my lawyer. Somebody stole my car." She gave him a withering look.

"Borrowed," he said. "I imagine Hal's already figured out when I got the keys copied. I noticed him in that cap and black shirt, lurking outside the hardware store. I hoped the tennis-racquet story might fool him."

"It'd take a better man than you to fool the Silver Fox."

Officer Bertram put down his ice pack and stood up. There was a noticeable red welt on his forehead. "I'd better have a word with Harmon," he said. "I suppose an apology is in order. I never believed he was up to any harm myself. He's been a model citizen ever since he came to Canada."

Sally and John followed him to the living room where the atmosphere had warmed up considerably. Martha was smiling, and Hal was looking triumphant.

"If someone was feeding secrets to the boys in the Middle East, it wasn't me," Hal said. "Mind you, I have a few ideas who might be responsible...."

"Then who is this Lottie Faraday, who was sending you tapes and asking for money?" Martha asked suspiciously.

Hal put his heads back and laughed. "One of my more eager fans. The head of my West Coast fan club, as it happens. The CIA will find her harmless, if a little flaky. She wanted me to put money into a music tape she's making. More important what did you do with the disk for *After the Storm?*"

"I sent it to CIA. I'll see that you get it back, if you want it. You said you were through with it. When I read that suggestive label, I thought it was your current spy project. That's why I took it."

"I guess we both said things we didn't mean," he replied. "That is the book I'm working on. The Japanese one was a ruse."

"I didn't fool you for a minute, did I? You saw right through me. You really should return to the department, Hal," Martha said. "It's criminal to let your expertise go to waste. No one knows the situation in the Middle East as intimately as you."

"I'm tempted," he said. "I admit I do miss the excitement. I've quite enjoyed this weekend. I'll think about it, Martha. But don't have Staynor call me—except to apologize. I'll call him, if I decide to return to the fold."

Mrs. Locum served coffee. The Mounties apologized to Harmon. John apologized, Martha apologized until Sally was tired of hearing it.

Eventually the Mounties left, and Sally said, "It's practically morning. Are we going back to Hilltop, Hal, or staying here?"

"We can't sleep two guests of the opposite sex here," Hal said.

"I'm sure the hotel could find rooms for them," Sally said.

"We'll all return to Hilltop. Martha has promised me a game of golf before she leaves tomorrow."

John looked uncertainly at Sally. "I'll go to the hotel if you don't want me—"

But she did want him—very much. "You might as well come back, too," she said with an indifferent shrug.

John gave a hopeful smile. She scowled. "We can have that game of tennis," he said. "There must be something I can beat you at."

"Don't count on it. And while I think of it, how about giving me back my keys? You must have driven ninety miles an hour. You've probably ruined my engine."

"That's only fair. You've ruined mine," he said, and handed her the keys.

"I always suspected you were a robot," she retorted, and they left. Hal drove Martha, leaving Sally and John to go together.

"So, why did you lie to me about working for Wigo?" she demanded. Sally drove, to show who was in charge.

"You suggested it. I hadn't a clue who Wigo was, and I could hardly announce who I really was."

"Big of you to agree to stop working for Wigo, when you never were working for them."

"I just wanted to ease your mind," he said.

"You wanted to keep me in the dark, you mean."

"I'm not the only one who did a little fiddling with the truth," he reminded her.

They drove home considerably more slowly than ninety miles an hour. Their bickering soon dwindled to silence. Since a light rain was falling, they couldn't put the top down, but it felt cozy with the raindrops pattering on the canvas roof while they were snug and warm inside. When they reached Hilltop, Hal's car was there already. Lights in the living room told them Hal and Martha were still up.

"I'm really sorry about all this, Sally," John said. "I felt terrible, having to deceive you."

"And you had the nerve to tell me I was spoiled. You thought I was working with Hal, doing it for the money. Is that it?"

"I did offer you an ear to confess in. I was willing to help you escape unscathed," he reminded her.

"I know. I was just working off my temper. Hal's spoken about the kind of work you do. You look for the weak link. You're not allowed to let your emotions get in the way. I understand, John. Anything to get the job done, even pretending you like your victim.

"I didn't have to pretend. And like isn't exactly the word I'd have chosen. I'd give anything if we could have met under other circumstances. After the way I've behaved, I can't ask you to forgive me. All I can say is, I'm sorry, Sally."

She cocked her head and smiled. "Did you ever see that movie, *Love Story?*"

"Yeah, I caught it on the late show last year. Terrific movie. The one with the famous line—"

"Love means never having to say you're sorry," she said, and looked at him invitingly.

His arm went around her shoulders. "Sally, are you saying what I think you're saying?"

"I'm just trying to find out whether you really have to say you're sorry."

His head lowered to hers. "No, I'm not sorry. I'm damned glad," he whispered, and brushed her lips gently. She remembered the kiss when she was in bed earlier, pretending to be asleep. She couldn't let herself respond then, but now her blood quickened, and her lips moved hungrily on his. He crushed her against him while the kiss escalated to scalding passion.

Overhead the rain pattered on the roof, but inside the car, the sun was shining. John kissed her thoroughly, then drew back and gazed at her. His face was a shadow, his eyes only a glitter in the darkness.

"It'll mean moving to Washington, Sally," he said. "New York was another lie. I can't give you all the things you have here. Not yet, anyway."

"Oh, John." She laughed. "What I have here is a selfish uncle and a nothing special job. Nine days out of ten I just type Hal's novels. I can get a job in Washington. You don't have to worry about me."

"I like worrying about you," he said. "And whether I like it or not, I can't seem to help doing it. If that isn't love... Shall we go and tell your uncle? Do you think he'll mind?"

"No. Anyway, it's my life. But let's go and tell him the news."

The hasty movement on the sofa told them that Hal and Martha had been making up in the time-honored fashion of a kiss. Hal said triumphantly, "We have a little announcement to make, folks. Martha has agreed to marry me. I've warned her of all the drawbacks. I'm old enough to be her fa—older brother. Staynor has talked me into doing a little job for him. Martha phoned him to demand he send that disk back as soon as possible. It's the middle of the night, but he deserves it, the hound. He apologized very nicely and insisted he needs me. I'll be selling the condo in Guelph, Sally. I'll keep the farm for the time being. You can live here. You won't have any trouble finding a job in Guelph.''

Sally just looked at John. "I guess he won't mind too much," she said. Then she turned to her uncle. "Piece of cake, Hal. We have an announcement also. John and I are getting married.''

Hal put his head back and laughed. "Congratulations, John. And all the best to you, my dear Sally. Life is strange indeed. Martha came to Canada to try to catch me in some act of treason and ended up falling in love with me. This is like one of your romances, Sal. John loves Sally. I picture it in my mind's eye as using a heart instead of the word 'loves,' as New York did in its advertising campaign, and the world has copied ad nauseam. Well, Hal loves Martha, too. Martha is actually Elizabeth Hanson, by the way. A biology major, which is why she was knowledgeable about fir trees.''

Sally went and put her arms around Martha. "Welcome to the family, Aunt Lizzie. I leave my uncle in your capable hands. Maybe we can go shopping for our trousseaux together.''

"I'd love it, Sally. Good heavens! I'll be your aunt!'' Elizabeth exclaimed and looked quite aghast to discover her niece-to-be was only ten years younger than herself.

"Elizabeth doesn't like to be called Lizzie, Sal,'' Hal said. "Don't let us detain you, dear,'' he added impatiently.

She saw that he wanted to be alone with Elizabeth. She and John went on upstairs.

"We won't make that tennis game too early, will we?" she said at her door, yawning into her fist.

"We don't have to bother playing. We already know the score. Love all."

"That's pretty corny, John."

"Yeah, but with a score like that, neither of us will have to say we're sorry."

"This goes from bad to worse."

"I'm on a roll. There's only one way to shut me up."

He pulled her into his arms and backed her against the wall. His wicked grin softened to love as he lowered his lips to hers and kissed her thoroughly. No words were spoken for some minutes. The only sound in the hallway was the sound of heavy breathing. But the echo of future wedding bells was not far off.

*   *   *   *   *

What a year for romance!

Silhouette has five fabulous romance collections coming your way in 1993. Written by popular Silhouette authors, each story is a sensuous tale of love and life—as only Silhouette can give you!

SPRING FANCY
Three bachelors are footloose and fancy-free...until now.
(March)

to Mother with Love
Heartwarming stories that celebrate the joy of motherhood.
(May)

SILHOUETTE SUMMER Sizzlers
Put some sizzle into your summer reading with three of Silhouette's hottest authors.
(June)

SILHOUETTE Shadows
Take a walk on the dark side of love—with tales just perfect for those misty autumn nights.
(October)

Silhouette CHRISTMAS Stories
Share in the joy of yuletide romance with four award-winning Silhouette authors.
(November)

Silhouette®

A romance for all seasons—it's always time for romance with Silhouette!

PROM93

Fifty red-blooded, white-hot, true-blue hunks from every
State in the Union!

Beginning in May, look for MEN MADE IN AMERICA!
Written by some of our most popular authors, these
stories feature fifty of the strongest, sexiest men, each
from a different state in the union!

Two titles available every other month at your favorite
retail outlet.

In September, look for:

DECEPTIONS by Annette Broadrick (California)
STORMWALKER by Dallas Schulze (Colorado)

In November, look for:

STRAIGHT FROM THE HEART by Barbara Delinsky
(Connecticut)
AUTHOR'S CHOICE by Elizabeth August (Delaware)

You won't be able to resist MEN MADE IN AMERICA!

Is your father a Fabulous Father?

Then enter him in Silhouette Romance's

"FATHER OF THE YEAR" Contest
and you can both win some great prizes! Look for contest details
in the FABULOUS FATHER titles available in June, July
and August...

ONE MAN'S VOW by Diana Whitney
Available in June

ACCIDENTAL DAD by Anne Peters
Available in July

INSTANT FATHER by Lucy Gordon
Available in August

Only from

Silhouette Books
is proud to present
our best authors,
their best books...
and the best in
your reading pleasure!

Throughout 1993, look for exciting
books by these top names in
contemporary romance:

DIANA PALMER—
Fire and Ice in June

ELIZABETH LOWELL—
Fever in July

CATHERINE COULTER—
Afterglow in August

LINDA HOWARD—
Come Lie With Me in September

When it comes to passion,
we wrote the book.

Silhouette®

DIANA PALMER
IS BACK!

and bringing you two more wonderful stories filled with love,
laughter and unforgettable passion. And this time, she's crossing
lines....

In August, Silhouette Desire brings you NIGHT OF LOVE (#799)

Man of the Month Steven Ryker promised to steer clear of his
ex-fiancée, Meg Shannon. but some promises were meant to
be broken!

And in November, Silhouette Romance presents KING'S RANSOM
(#971)

When a king in disguise is forced to hide out in Brianna Scott's
tiny apartment, "too close for comfort" gets a whole new meaning!

Don't miss these wonderful stories from bestselling author
DIANA PALMER. Only from ▼ *Silhouette*

DPTITLES